We're All Mad, You Know!

By

Gary McGuire

ISBN: 0-9652385-0-4

First Mary Lee Press printing: May 1996

10 9 8 7 6 5 4 3 2

Mary Lee Press
PO Box 295
Chandler, OK 74834

Printed in U.S.A.

We're All Mad, You Know!

Pararescue Running Chant

Hey, Hey, what do you say,
We're Pararescue all the way.
C-130 rollin' down the strip,
PJ Daddy gonna take a little trip.
Stand up, hook up, shuffle to the door,
Jump right out and count to four.
If my main don't open round,
Box me up when I hit the ground.
If my main don't open wide,
Just tell my folks how I died.

Dedication

For me, the story you will read in this book actually began with an Army patrol in Vietnam. Early one morning in 1971, a squad watched as another squad passed through their ambush zone to set up farther down-trail. When the passing squad disappeared toward their area of operations near a dried river embankment, all hell broke loose as they were in turn ambushed by the Vietcong.

The first squad, realizing their buddies were in trouble, ran to help. But before they could arrive, they in turn were ambushed and found themselves unable to move. With bullets kicking up dirt inches from their bodies, the squad members hugged the ground as best they could.

Someone managed to call in air support and helicopters arrived and began dropping white phosphorous grenades on the enemy positions. White flowering explosions filled the air as white-hot particles of burning phosphorous laced out to create havoc with the Vietcong.

Because of the nearness of the enemy, some of the phosphorous arced out and fell on American soldiers. Two soldiers were hit, setting their uniforms on fire. They jumped to their feet and began running around, screaming in pain as bullets continued to fill the air. Two men, one the squad leader, jumped up and tackled the two victims and rolled them to the ground extinguishing the flames. Immediately the squad leader picked up his casualty and began carrying him away from the ravine where the squad was trapped. The soldier who dove on the second man followed, carrying his casualty over his shoulder. But before he could reach the top of the ravine, he was struck by a bullet which knocked him out from underneath his casualty.

Writhing in pain, he watched his blood run from his wounded shoulder until it looked like it was running down the dried-up river bed. As he lay there bullets struck between his legs, near his head and to each side. Yet, the shoulder wound would miraculously be the only wound he would receive that fateful day.

The wounded soldier, medevaced five hours later, eventually beat the odds and regained almost full use of his arm. And it was because of this, among other things, that motivated me to join the Air Force, and eventually become a PJ.

The soldier is my brother, Frank. It's to him I dedicate this book.

I also wish to dedicate this writing to all PJs, past, present, and future, and;

To my son Merrick, so he'll better know his father;

To Dr. Robert Melton and Mary Samara for their help and encouragement while writing this book;

Major General Bob Walls (USAF Ret.), for all of your encouragement;

To my parents, Willie and Esabell, who believed I would one day finish this book;

To Mark Butterworth who opened the door for this manuscript to reach publication;

And most of all, to my wife, Mary Lee McGuire, without whose support and understanding, this book would never have been completed.

Contents

WE'RE ALL MAD, YOU KNOW

Introduction

In the annals of military history there has risen needs by military organizations to form highly trained groups and teams for specialized missions. The Marines have Force Recon, the Navy has its SEALs, and the Army its Rangers and Special Forces. All of these teams are trained and equipped for combat missions: to seek and find the enemy, then destroy him.

The U.S. Air Force also has a specialized team. But this team is not trained to find and kill. Instead, its mission is to save lives. No matter where, no matter the dangers involved. Whether the mission requires being lowered into a hostile area, while under fire, from a hovering helicopter, or parachuting into a storm-tossed ocean from a transport plane while wearing full SCUBA gear, the brave men of the Air Force Pararescue Team are always ready, willing and able.

To demonstrate the capabilities and courage of those in Pararescue--the "PJ's" as they are called--no mission illustrates this more than one that "went down" on October 3, 1993.

The place was Mogadishu, Somalia.

On that fateful date, members of Task Force Ranger received orders to attempt a "snatch" mission to capture militia leaders of Somalian war lord Mohamed Aideed. The location was a large building in downtown Mogadishu on Hiwadag Street.

As Task Force Ranger mounted up in their UH-60 Blackhawk helicopters, they were joined by two Air Force PJs: Master Sergeant Scott Fales and Tech Sergeant Timothy Wilkinson, and combat controller Staff Sergeant Jeffrey Bray. For the Army Rangers, the inclusion of these three men in the joint task force makeup would become most fortunate.

At 3 p.m. the snatch team loaded into the helicopters, Bray going in with the snatch team, and the two PJs in another aircraft that would hold nearby as a search and rescue ship. Within minutes they were airborne and enroute to the objective. Little did they realize that everything that could go wrong would, and the mission would not "end" for fifteen hours. They were about to be involved in the longest sustained firefight involving U.S. forces since the Vietnam war.

As the Rangers and Bray fast-roped from their hovering helicopter on Hiwadag Street, gunfire opened up all around them. Still, the mission continued and within minutes the Rangers managed to round up several militia suspects. During these tense minutes Bray took up a position in a doorway and began firing at gunmen in an alleyway. Quickly realizing they needed more firepower, Bray called in a gunship and directed supporting fire. Eventually, the team finished collecting the prisoners and was ready to evacuate the area by reaction force trucks that were to meet them nearby.

Then things went bad. One of the Blackhawks, call sign Super 61, was struck by an RPG-7 rocket-propelled grenade and went down with its crew and five passengers into a narrow alleyway 300 yards from Bray. The command-and-control bird radioed Bray to immediately move to the crash site.

Meanwhile, Pararescuemen Fales and Wilkinson, aboard their search and rescue chopper, call sign Super 68, which was in a holding pattern over a sports stadium, got the "one minute" call to go in. It was 3:39 p.m. and already casualties were mounting.

Fales and Wilkinson sat on opposite sides of the Blackhawk as it neared the deployment zone over Freedom Road. As the pilot pulled the aircraft to a hover, and a fifteen-man security team began fast-roping to the street below, the two PJs began throwing medical supplies, stretchers and ruck sacks to the ground. It was only after everyone was out and all gear deployed that the two men grabbed the ropes and started to descend to join the teams below.

At that moment the helicopter was struck with an RPG rocket just below the main rotor blades. But instead of transitioning to forward flight to escape the danger area, the pilots bravely held the hover until both PJs were safely on the ground.

Once on the deck, the PJs scrambled for cover amidst bursts of AK-47 fire. Fales and six companions began advancing along one side of the street while Wilkinson's group made their way along the other side. Within minutes Wilkinson's group had to cut across the street, dodging bursts of gunfire as they scrambled to join Fales.

While this was going on, Bray, now working with a Ranger platoon, managed to advance toward the crash site. As they leapfrogged in two elements, they engaged Somalis on parallel streets who were attempting to beat them to the downed chopper. The closer they got, the more resistance they met. Finally, as they neared the location of the wreckage, the gunfire became so intense that the team had to take cover and regroup. Bray located a small courtyard with metal grate doors. Throwing himself against the closed gates, he managed to force them open after repeated efforts. Once inside he immediately set up a casualty collection point.

It was now becoming evening, and Somalis swarmed around the trapped Rangers. The soldiers barricaded themselves in houses along Freedom Road, then began efforts to retrieve bodies of fallen comrades that littered the street.

As Bray was setting up his casualty collection point, Fales and Wilkinson were nearing the helicopter crash site. Each group made its way forward amidst automatic rifle fire, RPG rockets and hand grenades.

Fales made it to the wreckage first, followed a minute later by Wilkinson's group. They were too late to save the pilots, as both were dead in the cockpit. But one of the crew members was inside the wreckage of the troop compartment attempting to free the trapped crew chief. But before they could lend a hand, a bullet smacked into Fales' lower leg.

"It felt like someone took a hot poker and shoved it through my calf muscle," Fales recalled later. "I took my scissors out, cut my pants and saw what I had. I thought, 'Damn, this should hurt,' but it didn't."

Fales forced the muscle tissue back into his leg, packed it with gauze, then applied a battle dressing. As he was doing this, Wilkinson made his way to the nose of the helicopter where he helped a group of Rangers free one of the dead pilots from the twisted cockpit. Other Rangers helped Fales to the casualty collection point.

After removing the dead pilot, Wilkinson crawled into the fuselage and helped free the pinned crew chief.

As the shooting intensified, Wilkinson shoved the crew chief up and out of the wreckage to waiting Rangers and an Army medic. Just then small arms fire ripped through the fuselage, sending a piece of metal into Wilkinson's face and lower arm, and into the Army medic's hand.

Fales, now back at the wreckage, joined Wilkinson in treating the wounded at the tail of the aircraft. Rangers laid down covering fire as both men worked, since they were exposed to Somali fire. Just then the call for "medic!" filtered through the din of battle from the courtyard across the street. Wilkinson grabbed his medical bag and raced up the narrow alley after dashing some forty-five meters across open ground.

As soon as he arrived he began helping to drag wounded men off of Freedom Road to the casualty collection point. As he was completing this mission, he heard Fales ask for more medical supplies over their team radio. This required Wilkinson to again cross the danger area to the crash site. Army Ranger Captain Scott Miller later wrote: "It should be noted that these trips across the open street were at the peak of the battle when enemy fire was at its most intense. We were receiving intense and accurate small arms and RPG fire. His [Wilkinson's] acts of heroism saved the lives of at least four soldiers."

The trapped Rangers, outnumbered and outgunned, found their odds getting worse as the battle raged on into the night. Not expecting the mission to last this long, they had left their night vision goggles behind. Now the only way they could tell where the Somalis were moving and massing was by radio from NVG-equipped helicopter gunship crews.

Combat controller Bray was busy too. He repeatedly called in fire missions from the gunships, many times so close to the trapped groups that expended brass from the mini-guns showered down on their heads. In all, 60,000 rounds of ammo and 63 rockets were expended.

By this time Fales group had taken refuge in a nearby building, which was now becoming pounded by RPG rockets to the point it was near collapse. One of the Rangers had to blow a hole in a back wall to allow the trapped men to escape before they were annihilated.

They managed to evacuate everyone and move the wounded to another building, which they had to breach with explosives to gain entry. Just then a Somali heavy machine gun opened up and penetrated the walls with strings of bullets, every fifth round a tracer that lit the room like a dance floor strobe light.

The battle raged until 4 a.m. when Fales heard explosions and gunship fire approaching in the distance. It was the relief column that finally managed to fight its way through the streets, but only after highjacking some Pakistani tanks to lead the way. The American forces did not have tanks because the Secretary of Defense, Les Aspin, had decided they were not needed and showed too much of an unfriendly or warlike face for our "peace" mission.

Finally, the battle swept by as the relief force arrived at the crash site. Fales, Wilkinson and Bray were exhausted, suffered from dehydration, and for Fales, loss of blood. All were evacuated to the Olympic Hotel collection site by the relief column.

The battle was over. However, the cost of the mission was high. Task Force Ranger lost 18 soldiers, and had 84 wounded.

For their actions, Wilkinson was awarded the Air Force Cross for extraordinary heroism, and Bray and Fales received Silver Stars for gallantry.

What kind of men are these, who go into the den of the tiger without hesitation to help their fellow man? How are they selected, trained, and motivated?

That is the subject of this book, told through the story of one who made the grade as an Air Force Pararescue Jumper--a "PJ."

As you read what follows, you will come to understand why non-PJs all claim that those who go through what Gary McGuire did are "all mad, you know."

LTC Craig Roberts (USAR)

Author of:
The Walking Dead: A Marine's Story of Vietnam

One Shot--One Kill: America's Combat Snipers

Combat Medic--Vietnam

Police Sniper

Prologue

By
Major General Bobby E. Walls, USAF (Ret)

I never really knew the rigourous training the PJ recruits had to undergo just to become qualified in the art of rescue. I hesitate to say "fully qualified," because when does one ever become "fully qualified" in such a field? Much like doctors or lawyers that have practices, the PJs are constantly undergoing training to become more proficient in their field.

I am quite certain that everyone reading this book has seen documentaries showing PJs in action. Remember our early ventures into space? The people that jumped from the helicopters into the water to fasten bouyancy devices onto the space capsules were Pararescue members. I am certain that "Gus" Grissom was extremely happy to see their smiling faces when they greeted him after his landing in the Pacific Ocean. The hatch blew off the capsule that Gus was in after landing in the turbulent water. Had it not been for the PJs' quick and daring rescue, Gus would have been lost, along with his capsule.

I am also certain many have seen the films depicting the gallant rescue work of the PJs in Southeast Asia. The one that immediately comes to mind is the scene in the movie *Flight of the Intruder*. Almost all of the aircrew members that ejected during the Vietnam War were injured, either from enemy fire or during the ejection, opening of the chute, or landing phase after ejection. This movie shows quite clearly how the PJs jump onto a steel cable, with a jungle penetrator attached, to descend into the thick Vietnamese jungle to come to the aid of an injured aircrew member. All this with enemy bullets whining around them like angry wasps. Many of the aircrew would not have survived had it not been for the courage of the PJs. They would have died, or worse, have spent years in the Hanoi Hilton as prisoners of war. In all, the PJs were directly responsible for 3,383 "saves" during the war in Vietnam.

I, as a fighter pilot, quite thankfully, never had to call upon these courageous people to come to my rescue. I was very fortunate, but many of my friends did prevail upon the PJs and their daring deeds. All of them were ready and eager to buy them a drink at the first opportunity. One friend in particular bailed out over the waters off Korea. He hit the frigid water, went under, and when he surfaced, the cable and sling were right by his head. All he had to do was grab it, climb in, and be hoisted aboard. Talk about good service!

The only time I thought I could use a PJ was over the Gulf of Mexico. I had an A-7 aircraft trying to shake itself to pieces, and had I been able to swim, I might possibly have jettisoned from the aircraft. At the time I know that I would have been more than elated to see one or two of these people jumping into the waters of the Gulf to save my life.

We're All Mad, You Know tells a very vivid story of the type of individual that it takes to even attempt to become a member of this elite organization, and explains in detail just how demanding the training is. Being a fighter pilot is more a state of mind than of having extraordinary skills. One has to be aggressive and be an individualist. Much the same can be said of the USAF Pararescue personnel--our PJs.

Preface

0200 hours

1,000 feet over the South China Sea, somewhere off Subic Bay, the Philippines....

I stood in the open door of a rumbling C-130 rescue plane, staring down at the inky blackness of the ocean below. I managed to get set just as the jumpmaster slapped me on the thigh. I hesitated, it just didn't feel right. I reset myself and jumped with all my might into the windy darkness.

I looked up at the ghostly image of my parachute being blown past me by the prop wash. I already had twists in my suspension lines, from the risers just over my head to nearly the skirt of the canopy. It's called a cigarette roll, and I was building speed fast. I grabbed the risers and pulled them apart while I "bicycled" my legs.

I finally stopped spinning and the twists began to unwind. "This is taking entirely too long," I thought to myself, deciding to deploy my reserve. I tried to hold the pack closed as I pulled the rip cord handle so that I could grab some parachute and throw it out and away from my body. It didn't work. The spring loaded pilot chute got away from me catching air as I fell out from under it. A giant white cloud of parachute whizzed by only inches from my face, but instead of billowing out and stopping my fall, it wrapped around my main 'chute' from the spin of the untwisting suspension lines.

I looked out into the void. "Next time," I told myself, "I gotta remember to eject my main before I deploy the reserve." An overwhelming sensation of calm came over me and a warm wave flowed through my body. Seemed like it was taking a long time. "What's it going to be like?" I wondered.

If it's true that your life passes before your eyes before you die, here is what I should have seen.

Chapter One

Not About Basics

I left Oklahoma City as a brand new Air Force recruit on a cold day in early January, 1972 on an airplane bound for Lackland AFB, San Antonio, Texas. The plane was almost full of young men with the same destination, which was probably the only thing we all had in common. The remaining seats were filled during our stop over in Dallas and on the continuing flight we took advantage of the two cocktails we were allowed.

Three buses were waiting to transport us to Lackland. This is the only base where the Air Force trains basic recruits. Our driver, a civilian, assured us that we wouldn't be allowed to smoke until after the first week. "So," he told us, "if you smoke you had better do it now." We chain

1

smoked the rest of the way in, and come to find out he was telling the truth. I should have taken advantage of the situation and quit.

"All right you 'rainbows,'" a sergeant shouted as we got off the bus, "line up on the pad." The pad was a cement slab under the overhang of the three story barracks that we lived in for the next six weeks. They were so new that only a few training flights had occupied them before us. We were called "rainbows" because of the variety of colors of our hair and civilian clothing. But we didn't stay rainbows very long.

After four days of marching, "hurry-up-and-wait," and folding our underwear just right, we were finally marched to a large building where it was decided what we would be as GIs. After seven hours of listening to lectures, watching films and filling out forms, my four choices boiled down to either mechanic, cook, military police or linguistics. I chose linguistics because I didn't know what the hell it was, but it sounded important.

We turned our forms in and time was running out when we were greeted by a lovely, almost sensuous WAF who informed us we had one other choice of career that was not mentioned earlier because it was totally voluntary.

"It's called Pararescue," she told us. "You will be medically trained to save lives. You'll be trained to make parachute jumps, to operate self contained underwater breathing apparatus, climb mountains, and survive in hostile environments."

She paused for a moment looking at us seductively before continuing, "Besides all that, the women just love the cute little maroon beret you'll wear."

2

WE'RE ALL MAD, YOU KNOW

That was all she needed to say. Immediately most all of us raised our hands. We signed the volunteer forms and were given passes to attend a pre-screening briefing to be held later in the week.

Several hundred volunteers met back at the same building on the evening of the briefing. I couldn't help but overhear some of the people bragging on themselves while we waited for something to happen. I sat quietly by myself in the back row not wanting to be conspicuous. An eerie silence fell over the room when in walked one of the meanest looking men I had ever seen. He was six feet tall weighing nearly one hundred-ninety pounds. His entire mannerism was one of authority, and the only sound to break the silence was his highly spit-shined jump boots striking the floor as he marched up to the podium. The uniform he wore belonged exclusively to Pararescue. His dress blue slacks stopped at the top of his bloused jump boots. Above his left pocket he wore six rows of ribbons, with parachute jump wings above the ribbons and flight crew member wings above that. This, I told myself, was the image of what I wanted to be.

He took off his beret and placed it on the podium as he slowly scanned his audience. In an extremely matter-of-fact tone he began asking a series of questions. "Is there anyone in here that wears glasses or contact lenses?"

Quite a few people raised their hands and to those he nodded toward the door and said, "You must have twenty-twenty vision to be on flight status. You people can go."

He waited for them all to leave before asking if anyone had been convicted of a felony. A few lads got up and left without being told to do so. Still more people left as he asked if anyone had a history of asthma, rheumatic fever, scoliosis, mental disorders and more on his long list of medical problems. He wasn't showing any emotion up to the time he ran out of disqualifying questions to ask and he spent a few more moments looking at those of us remaining.

"My name is Technical Sergeant Colvert." He managed a smile as he congratulated us for being eligible to try for his elite group of "PJs" as they liked to be called. He told us only three hundred thirteen PJs were on active duty at any one time around the world but not to let that discourage us because every one of us could make the team if we just had what it took to stay with it.

He was giving us a great pep talk and we were all taken in by his friendly, persuasive personality when he concluded by saying, ."...so it's true that we PJs work very hard but it is also true that we party just as hard. Why, I remember one party I was at and I mean there were women and we were smoking pot; some of you do smoke pot, don't you?"

Six hands went up in the air in the momentum of the moment and you could see the smile on his face turn into a menacing frown as he screamed, "Get out of my briefing, *now*!"

It would be three months before I would see a smile on his face again.

By now only a quarter of the original crowd remained, maybe fifty or so. We were shown a film that was taken of a PJ training class running around a track while the narrator told a short history of Pararescue. It took a few years for this small team of highly trained professionals to evolve into the complex crews that are flying today. In early 1966, an act by then Air Force Chief of Staff, General John P. McConnell, allowed the unique uniform and maroon beret to be worn by these special force paramedics. Maroon was chosen to signify the blood of the fallen heroes in the line of duty and a motto was written, "These things we do; that others may live."

The film reiterated the training that the WAF sergeant described the week before except that she failed to mention the running and exercises that would be required of us. Colvert told us before the film started to feel free to leave at any point if we felt we would not be able to complete the vigorous physical training, or "PT," as he referred to it. Every few minutes someone would up and head for the door until only a few minutes of the film remained. When it was over there couldn't have been more than twelve of us left for Colvert to look over. He handed each of us a pass to take to our basic instructor so that in two weeks, on a Saturday morning, we could all meet at the PJ barracks for a physical ability test.

"A word to the wise," Colvert said as he watched us leave the room, "practice your push-ups."

As I walked to the barracks I wondered what made me think I had the stuff it took to not only endure the day-to-day routine, but to actually jump out of a perfectly good airplane. In high school I had swam the four hundred yard free style for the swim team, but was never good enough to come in better than third place. And even though I ran with the cross country team, of fifty kids I busted my ass to finish twentieth. The only reason the coach lettered me

5

in swimming in my senior year was because he felt sorry for me. That and the fact I was always there and trying.

My interest in water as a sport led me on what seemed a natural course of events that went from becoming a certified life guard to sport SCUBA diving. After becoming SCUBA certified I joined the Oklahoma Hydronauts, a local diving club, and was an assistant instructor at the time I joined the Air Force. It had been a little over a year since I had done any serious exercising and now I had two weeks to get ready for whatever it was that Colvert had in mind for me.

Practice my push-ups I did, or at least I thought I did. Each night in the barracks I went into the back room and did a few sets of twenty thinking I was really doing something. A couple of my friends joined me to keep me company but even they thought I was having visions of grandeur. Everyone else was laughing at me behind my back.

That long awaited Saturday morning finally arrived. I was up at 0600 to get dressed before stopping at the chow hall for breakfast. Even south Texas gets cold in late January and as I walked the mile and a half across base in the twenty six degree pre-dawn weather, my only thoughts were on how badly I wanted this.

The only directions I had received regarding where to report for this test was the barracks number. I simply walked in what I thought was the right direction until I found the number. The barracks were World War II vintage and for a few minutes I stood outside looking at them wondering if I might be on the wrong side of the base. If so it was too late now because it was 0800 and this was the time we were all supposed to meet. Just then, eight guys wearing sweat tops and bottoms and green tennis shoes came out the barracks doors, and two at a time jumped up on the pull-up bar that crossed the walk in front of the door. They each did ten pull-ups plus one more yelling, "One for Pararescue," as they did it.

When they all finished the pull-ups, they lined up in two columns, four deep. The apparent leader ordered, "Forward by the double time, march!"

Each man stepped off with his left foot first in a quick paced run singing, "Rescue, rescue, all the way, rescue rescue all the way. We like it here, we like it here, we finally found a home. We like it here, we like it here, we finally found a home."

I watched as they ran around a corner and out of sight. The song they were singing changed but continued and trailed off in the distance. They were so pre-occupied with what they were doing that they paid no attention to my presence.

One other volunteer out of the twelve that had passed pre-screening with me walked up saying he wasn't sure where he was supposed to be until he saw those guys running by. He then backtracked them to this barrack row.

As we chatted for a moment, a leaner sergeant than Colvert came out of the building wearing jungle fatigues bloused above his jump boots. As he stepped out of the door he began pulling his maroon beret over his short-cropped head, looking our way. "I didn't think anybody was going to show up this morning."

He walked up to us. "I'm sergeant Kee." He offered his hand, and I shook it as I introduced myself saying, "Hello,

7

I'm Airman McGuire." The other airman did the same and we turned to walk with him, following slightly behind.

"Enjoy the walk," he told us along the way, "because once you move in, you'll run everywhere you go or you don't go at all. Every time you go in or out of the barracks, you'll do ten pull-ups and no matter which exercise you're doing, you will always do one more for Pararescue." That explained the behavior of the earlier group of trainees.

Our destination turned out to be the "training pool." The pool was small, only twenty five yards long and ten yards wide. Although it was outside, the thick layer of fog drifting across the surface told me it was heated.

"Get changed and we'll get started," ordered Kee.

We changed clothes in the locker room into the swimming trunks we had been told to bring. Kee quickly told us we had one hour to swim twenty four laps around the pool, which was close to a mile. Large goose pimples had bulged out of my skin by the time I hit the warm water of the pool. It took forty-five minutes to complete the mile, my companion finished five minutes behind me. We hustled back to the locker room to change back into our fatigues and boots to escape the freezing cold.

Going out again by the side of the pool we were told to knock out twenty-five push-ups, which we did with a minimal amount of effort. I knew something was wrong as we finished doing fifty sit-ups because this was just too easy. He told us to do twenty-five flutter kicks but I had to confess that I didn't know what a flutter kick was.

Kee laid down on his back to demonstrate, putting his fist under the cheeks of his butt and raised his legs six inches off the ground. "This is the beginning and ending position," he said. "Always start with the left leg raising it as high as you can stretch it and count one. As you lower the left leg, raise your right leg at the same time and count two, repeating left and right counting three with the left and the number of repetitions with the right. You do not have to use the four count now but once you move in, every exercise, with rare exceptions will be four count." He got up after doing ten or so and now it was our turn. By twenty, my boots were so heavy I couldn't keep my legs straight and at twenty five the pain in my abdomen was a burning cramp. He had us hold our legs out as straight as we could for another ten seconds before he let us get up. It took a minute for me to be able to stand straight again.

"It would behoove you to practice these exercises in your spare time," Kee said as if it were a hint.

We left the pool and walked to the quarter mile, oval track where we had eight minutes to run a mile. It proved to be no serious effort and we walked in silence back to the barracks. We did ten pull-ups in front of the barracks for him and he turned to go inside. The two of us stood there not knowing what to do next.

As if to answer our question, Kee turned back around saying, "The day you get out of basic, bring your duffel bags and move in here." He went inside leaving us alone.

That was the entire test. We walked only a few steps when we heard the faint sound of singing off in the distance. The sound was growing steadily louder so we moved off the sidewalk to wait for them.

"Man," I was thinking to myself, "if that test was any indication of what was to come, then this is going to be easier than I thought."

The team turned the corner and ran down the sidewalk toward the barracks. As they passed in front of us the leader ordered, "Route step, March!"

On the next left foot they broke rank with the two lead people going to the pull-up bar, doing their ten-plus-one and hustled off the bar. The next set of two men were on the bar immediately behind them until they all finished and disappeared into the barracks. Again they paid no attention to my presence.

I thought about the look on their faces as they ran by with mouths agape, eyes widened and sweat soaking through their clothes. What the hell had those eight guys been doing?

As a basic recruit we were required to call everybody with one stripe or more "sir". This caused me some trouble later. My basic training instructor laughed uncontrollably upon learning of my acceptance into Pararescue training.

"Your as good as dead right now," he said. "A PJ's life expectancy in combat is about thirteen seconds--and not much better in peace time. The only people with worse odds than you are test pilots." He was still laughing when he left the room.

No one believed I would even last a week much less complete the training. I had some doubts myself but I wasn't going to let anybody else know that. My determination only made them laugh more.

10

WE'RE ALL MAD, YOU KNOW

A week before graduation from basic we were marched to an area where everyone was issued their orders for whatever technical school they were to attend. A sergeant called out the names on the orders and the recipients walked up to receive them. I began to wonder if he was going to call my name, and sure enough when he finished he asked if there was anyone whose name he did not call. I was the only one that raised a hand.

"What did you do?" he asked me after rechecking his list for my name. "Did you do something stupid like volunteer for something?"

"Yes sir, I volunteered for Pararescue."

He laughed before he told me that I didn't get any orders. "Just report to the sergeant at the Pararescue barracks when you get out of basic."

I was getting tired of being laughed at.

Air Force basic training is six weeks long and is the easiest of any branch of the service. Only the Marine Corps can change branches of service without repeating the monotony of basic training. Some people actually served in all four branches of the military during their twenty year career. I did not know yet that I was about to experience them all in less than one year.

On February 14th, 1972, Valentines Day, I graduated from basic training. My family hoped I could take a few days leave and go home to visit them. It would be eleven months before I saw home, family, and friends.

Chapter Two

Pre-Conditioning

The bus ride across base took over a half hour with a stop at every corner in between. Most of the GIs got off at the same stop I did. They were entering a phase called Casual, this means their Technical School would not be starting for a few days to a few weeks so they did odd jobs around the base. Their barracks were across from the PJs.

I mingled around with them for twenty minutes or longer starring across the way trying to imagine what it was going to be like. I wasn't in any kind of hurry, but eventually I made my way in that direction. "Hey you!" a two-striper yelled at me. "Only PJ trainees are allowed on that ground!"

WE'RE ALL MAD, YOU KNOW

"Is that a fact?" I yelled back to him. I'm sure I sounded arrogant, but fear was what I felt. He didn't say anything else as I turned to enter the two story barracks. When I got to the pull-up bar, I dropped my duffel bags and knocked out ten plus one for Pararescue. The bottom floor of the barracks was unoccupied. A stairway turned left then went up. At the top of the stairs, through the window in the door, I could see Sergeant Colvert. He was sitting behind his desk talking on the phone. He paused there long enough to yell, "The grounds outside need policing. Leave your bags here. You can unpack when you're done. Get out of my sight!"

I left without saying a word, did my pull-ups and started picking up loose paper and cigarette butts. The same two-striper was still outside trying to organize all the incoming Basic Training graduates. He was intentionally ignoring me.

Rick Prado, a PJ trainee, ran up to the barracks and was stopped at the door by sergeant Kee. The short conversation was inaudible, but I heard the sergeant order, "Drop!" Prado's feet slid back as his torso plummeted forward. He broke his fall only slightly with his hands and started doing push-ups, counting out loud. Kee noticed I was standing in the lawn watching.

"What the hell do you think you're doing?" he yelled. I didn't know "what the hell" I was doing and shrugged my shoulders at him.

"Drop!" he screamed at me, and I fell to the ground to do push-ups. When Prado finished, both he and Kee went upstairs leaving me alone again. Not knowing how many to do, I got up, picked up a few more cigarette butts and went inside.

Colvert's desk was vacant when I picked up my duffel bags. Two hallways entered the office from east and west. I had picked the east wing and started in that direction looking for a room. Almost immediately I ran into another PJ trainee who introduced himself bluntly.

"I'm Mike Carpenter," he said as he was coming out of his room. "This is class 72-04 and I'm the class leader. The best way to get along here is to do what you're told, when you're told, and keep your mouth shut."

I hadn't said a word yet so I thought I must be getting along. "You're in room eight. Spit shine it after you get unpacked and I suggest you get to bed early tonight." He went on in to the office and I went to my room.

I was placing my clothes in exactly the right position, the correct distance apart, and folded to the exact size just like I was taught to do in basic. Before I finished, Carpenter opened my door.

"Sergeant Kee wants to see you now," he said and left as suddenly as he came. Kee didn't seem to fit because he was not an ass. He was polite, friendly and just a matter-of-fact kind of guy.

"Airman McGuire reporting for duty as ordered, sir," I said as I snapped to attention in front of his desk and saluted.

"I'm a sergeant," he replied. "You do not call sergeants 'sir' and you do not salute them. Didn't you learn anything in basic?"

I lowered my hand but stayed at attention until he told me to stand at parade rest. His speech continued, "This is

14

WE'RE ALL MAD, YOU KNOW

a team, McGuire. There are no individuals. If one man is in trouble and does push-ups, the whole team is in trouble and does push-ups. When you drop, you do thirty-five but do not recover until you are told to do so. If you cannot complete the set non-stop, you can use the leaning rest before continuing. Do you have any questions?"

"I don't know what a leaning rest is," I confessed.

"Assume the push-up position," Kee told me, and I did. "That is a leaning rest. You can arch your back, lift a leg or an arm and shake them out but you cannot let your knees or stomach touch the ground. If either myself or sergeant Colvert catches you laying down, you're out."

Colvert had walked up, but from my position all I could see were his boots. "Because you called me 'sir,' you owe me thirty-five. So knock them out," Sergeant Kee ordered and I started doing Push-ups. "Start over," Kee said, "and this time count out loud."

"One, two, three," I yelled out loud and from both ends of the hall I heard everybody counting out push-ups. Colvert got down on his hands and knees to look at the space between my chest and the floor.

"Stop," he ordered. "Who do you think you're kidding. Hit my hand." He then placed his hand under my chest palm down on the floor. "You're not going all the way up. Lock your arms!" The additional effort it took to lower and raise myself those few extra inches was tremendous. These were the first real pushups I had ever done.

When the team yelled, "One for Pararescue," I was just reaching twenty-five and couldn't do anymore. I used the leaning rest like he told me and was able to do seven more before hitting the leaning rest again. I knocked out the last

15

three-and-one for Pararescue before he told everyone to recover. A resounding, "Hoo ya!" thundered through the barracks as everyone got up.

I was sweating and my arms and legs were weak as Kee continued to talk to me. "You must never quit because when you do you're out, and that's final. There are no second chances around here. We expect it to take you a week, or in your case maybe two, to be able to keep up with the exercises. So keep trying and don't quit. However, we do expect you to stay in step on the runs from day one. Airman Carpenter is the class leader, he'll fit you for your sweat gear and fill you in on the details. You're dismissed."

"Yes sir!" I answered before I gave myself time to think. I cringed from what I knew was coming.

"What?" he yelled. "Drop!"

I fell back to the floor counting out push-ups again along with everybody else in the barracks. Colvert walked up and down the hall to make sure no one was cheating. This time I was only able to do twenty before relying on the leaning rest to save me. The team finished with one for Pararescue while I was still shaking out my legs and they were all told to recover. Both Kee and Colvert were standing over me as I did a few at a time between stops in the leaning rest.

"You didn't practice, did you?" Colvert asked.

I was at number thirty with sweat dripping off my nose and my arms quivering with exhaustion, "No sergeant," I replied, making damn sure I didn't say "sir" again. I wiggled and squirmed one push-up at a time until the magic number thirty-five plus one for Pararescue finally came.

16

WE'RE ALL MAD, YOU KNOW

"Recover," Kee said the instant I finished. "Get out of here and square your room away." I left without saying a word.

Carpenter found a size small sweat suit for me. I only weighed one hundred forty pounds at 5'9." By 2100 hours I had stenciled 72-04, and my last name on the back of the sweat top, and had my room what I thought was inspection-ready before going to bed.

The light came on in my room waking me up and I saw Carpenter standing in the doorway. "Get up McGuire, it's 0500. You're responsible for waxing and buffing the hall and you better hurry because everybody has to wax and buff their rooms plus do their other chores before inspection at 0800."

Everybody was busy doing something. I opened a can of paste wax that Carpenter had given me, and taking a rag, I spread a coat over the hardwood floor of the hall. By 0745 everything in the entire barracks had been dusted, shined and polished down to each individual slat of all the Venetian blinds throughout the barracks.

Getting dressed each morning was a ritual in itself. Clean shorts and T-shirt and, "breaking starch." We had to have our fatigues starched extra heavy which stuck the material together so hard that we had to push our arms and legs through, thus the expression breaking starch. We were issued Red Wing jump boots and paid 75 cents at the barber every other day to have them polished to a glassy shine. On the in-between days it only took twenty minutes with a cotton ball, a little water and some polish to have them inspection ready. Using the little bungie cord called a "blousing band," we turned the pants legs under at the top of the boot. But were only allowed to blouse them this way while in fatigues. A "dickey", or Ascot was worn around our necks. The dark blue of the dickey that filled the space from the chin to the top button of the fatigue shirt gave the uniform a look of uniqueness.

At 0800 Colvert entered the barracks. Everyone was standing at attention outside the door of their rooms with somber expressions, many that bordered on fright. The inspection started at the opposite end of the barracks where the team I saw a month earlier lived. We couldn't see what was going on down there, but we had no trouble hearing Colvert yell "drop" not very long after he began. I was playing it by ear and followed everyone else's lead as they fell to the floor with their legs up to their waist inside their rooms with the rest of their trunk extending into the hall. That gave Colvert a clear view of us all from anywhere he was.

I stayed with the count up to twenty before I started falling behind, while everyone else stayed with the pace. By the time I reached one for Pararescue he had already found reason to make us drop again. He hadn't even let us recover and I struggled to do as many as I could as often as I could. Most of the team was knocking them out in rapid strokes but some of the others were showing signs of pain.

I had not quite finished thirty-six when he told us to recover, but I got up with everybody just the same. The old team had been there long enough to know what Colvert was looking for so we didn't have to drop too many times of their account. They, on the other hand, had

18

to drop many times on our account. I was astounded by how long this went on and how much people could sweat. Pools formed under our faces and the heavy starch was sagging with moisture by the tenth or so time we dropped. That didn't mean it was about to end, he was still five doors down from me and yelling "drop!" Everyone was in pain but surely mine was the worst. My muscles quivered uncontrollably and had to spend most of the time in a sloppy leaning rest but would attempt a few when I thought he was looking. We often did three sets between being allowed to recover, although two was common.

I was at attention when he walked up to me. He looked me over for a long moment, glanced into my room, then started yelling. "You're a pig living in a sty, McGuire. You better shape up fast or you're out!" He turned to the next room as if he didn't want to waste any more of his time on me.

We dropped one more time for some minor infraction as Colvert walked back to his office avoiding the pools of sweat. The last thing he told us before closing the door was to recover. My arms and legs felt like rubber as Carpenter announced to be ready for PT in ten minutes.

We walked downstairs to the basement and lined the walls in a circle with Carpenter in the center. We stood at attention wearing our sweats and green tennis shoes. This is where the future PJ was separated from the 'want-to-be'. Although we did only a dozen different exercises, the pace was fast and furious. The number of four-count repetitions was staggering. I started falling behind early, singling me out to Carpenter, and inviting his wrath. "You're never going to make it, McGuire", he told me. "Pick it up." My arms and legs quivered like Jello. I was soaked in sweat. On the seventy-fifth flutter kick, the pain was excruciating and I had to let my stomach rest. My feet hit the ground.

Carpenter looked as if he were going to explode. "Do you want to pack your bags right now, McGuire? Get 'em up or get out."

The eight men from the old class moved with the precision of a machine. These guys were some kind of tough. I looked like a dying cockroach. Key was giving me two weeks instead of the usual one to keep up. I was going to need every day of it.

"Forward, by the double time," Carpenter yelled and we responded with a chorus of "Who We Are" and "Blood And Guts" before he gave the order to "March." We were being led straight to the track from the basement, with a stop at the pull-up bar. The "We Like It Here" song always started as soon as our first left foot hit the ground. We ran in such a tight formation that if the lead people ever got out of step we would all stumble and fall all over each other but that never happened. No doubt that's why I ran in the back because I was out of step more often than not. The songs we sang were non-stop and as soon as the "We Like it Here" song ended, Carpenter would lead with a verse solo and the rest of us would repeat it. We sang to keep cadence with our left feet hitting the ground to the rhythm of modified Ranger songs. Only I was not singing with them. It took all the effort I could muster just to keep up, much less sing. These guys ran at a constant pace of seven minutes per mile which is a healthy clip by itself, and I didn't have any extra air to sing with. I felt myself catch my second wind after a mile and attempted a few verses. That was a drastic mistake. It drained what little strength I had left, and I started falling behind by a few inches with each stride. A stabbing pain shot through my sides. In reflex I bent over at the waist tucking my elbows into my gut running more in a wobble than a straight line, much less being in formation. Something unusual happens when you push yourself to unreasonable limits. It's difficult to describe, but its like a semiconscious state of mind. Legs, trunk and arms become numb and I was able to stand upright again. It felt like my body didn't belong to my mind anymore. Only the rhythmic pounding of the track under my feet reminded me that this was real. Maybe you would call it a "third" wind.

That's not to say it was easy. I briefly thought how easy it would be to justify quitting and honestly did not know if I could make another mile. I made up some of the distance I lost on the next quarter and caused the pain to return, driving me into agony under the sweat on my face.

"Drop out at the end of this quarter," Carpenter yelled back to me. I was being allowed to stop a half mile short because it was my first run. Carpenter saved my ass that day because he knew I couldn't finish the run. He was later called on the carpet by Colvert and was given a ration of shit for going easy on me. It then became a personal vendetta of Carpenter's to wash me out.

The team finished the run and I fell in at the rear to run with them back to the barracks. As I waited my turn on the pull-up bar I remembered the look on the faces of these same eight guys a month earlier. The thought sunk in that I had this to look forward to for a very long time. There was no order in who went to the pull-up bar first because nobody went inside until the last person (me) was done.

The time on the clock in the office said 1115 hours. We had spent less than thirty minutes outside so that meant we were downstairs for over two hours. Having it over should have felt good, but it hurt too much.

"You have thirty minutes, McGuire, to shower and dress for chow." Carpenter was giving me the details one at a time as they came up.

Thirty minutes was not a minute too long and I stuffed the dickey into the top of my shirt as I walked down the stairs, last again. I was determined not to be last very long. I did my pull-ups, fell in line and thanked God the chow hall was only down the street. We ate in leisurely comfort in no hurry to return. When we did decide to leave we fell in outside and ran back to the barracks, did our pull-ups and went inside. Carpenter told us at the top of the stairs to fall out for PT in ten minutes. I felt my gut turn and went to the latrine.

I entered my room to find I had a new roommate. He asked how things were around here. I told him only that he would find out soon enough and changed into my PT gear thinking I was going to be late. Everyone else was downstairs and my turn on the pull-up bar was next. After taking my place in line I noticed that Carpenter was carrying a basketball and much to my relief, we played an easy game for about an hour before returning.

The rest of the day was free time and we spent it taking dirty fatigues to the laundry, getting hair cuts, having boots shined and in my case buying a dickey and blousing bands. I picked up one pair of fatigues with extra heavy starch from the laundry that they prepared for me on an emergency basis so I would be ready for inspection in the morning. By 2000 hours I was in bed and asleep.

"Turn out the damn light," I said thinking it was my roommate getting ready for bed. "Get your ass up McGuire!" It was Carpenter and worse yet it was 0500. My body was as stiff as the starch in my fatigues and today was going to be no easier. My roommate was energetic and cleaned and polished everything with vigor. "There won't be anything wrong with this room," he said with pride as we stood at attention waiting for Colvert to arrive.

From the time Colvert entered the barracks to the time he yelled "drop" was not very long. My stiff body and sore arms loosened up during the first set and made it all the way to thirty before using the leaning rest. My roommate and I struggled to finish but we were not fast enough as Colvert yelled drop again. My roommate kept trying to pump them out even when Colvert was obviously out of sight.

"Save some strength for when he's watching," I whispered to him. "This goes on for a while."

It was a long while before Colvert made his way to our room. Something about me disgusted him, and without any reason he shouted in my face to "drop!" By the fifteenth repitition neither my roommate nor I could do any more.

Colvert shook his head and went inside our room. We hadn't finished the set when he screamed, "Get your butts in here!" I suppose he didn't want to wait that long.

"This is the filthiest room I've ever seen," Colvert declared. He put on a white glove and ran a finger across a panel of the venison blind.

23

"Look," he said showing us the speck of dust that collected. He violently jerked the bunk bed away from the wall and ran a different finger along the base board.

"Look!" he yelled as he showed us more dust. He pulled the locker away from the wall and found more dust. He grabbed a chair and threw it against the locker, stood on it and ran the palm of the gloved hand across the top. Stepping off the chair, he walked up to me and stuck a soiled palm in my face screaming, "You're a slob McGuire. A weak filthy slob and I do not want you doing my job. Drop!"

We fell to the floor knocking out push-ups only inches from his feet. When I stopped in the leaning rest after twenty he slid a form under my face. It read simply that the undersigned voluntarily withdraws from Pararescue training.

I did more push-ups.

"Sign the paper," Colvert said in a calm voice. I did more push-ups. "Sign the damned paper McGuire!" he screamed at me.

"No sergeant," I yelled back, completing the last push-up screaming, "One for Pararescue!"

"Recover!" he ordered, bending down to pick up the unsigned form as I struggled to my feet. "This room better be ready for inspection tomorrow," he said as if it were a warning. He left the room shaking his head.

My roommate looked at me with sweat dripping into his eyes. He didn't have time to say anything because Colvert had just yelled "drop" from the room across the hall. During a stop in the leaning rest my roommate said what was on his mind, "I'll be glad when this is over."

WE'RE ALL MAD, YOU KNOW

"No you won't," I replied. "It gets worse."

We recovered on Colvert's command from his office door and I started getting undressed even before Carpenter declared, "PT in ten minutes."

The routine was the same but my performance was not. I did even worse, but refused to quit. My roommate didn't seem to have the determination and collapsed to the floor several times. This made Carpenter extremely irate. I was, however, thankful for having the monkey off my back.

During the four count flutter kicks, my roommate let his legs fall to the floor and refused to pick them back up. He laid there for a moment weeping uncontrollably repeating, "I can't, I can't, I can't."

He was not the only man I saw break that way. As pathetic as the sight was, no one made fun of him or felt sorry for him. He left the basement room still crying while we continued.

The run was as difficult as the day before, and even worse because I had to finish with the team instead of stopping a half mile early. I made no attempt to sing cadence, concentrating only on staying in step. When I returned to my room after the pull-ups, there was no sign of my roommate ever having been there.

I never even knew his name.

Every couple of days someone new was moving in, and every couple of days someone was moving out. Most were like my first roommate, not completing the first PT, while others lasted for two, sometimes three days then packed their bags after learning that they would be here for two months or longer. I was surprised by how easily the

25

toughest looking guys quit, while the leaner, meeker guys like myself stayed with it. The faces changed so often that I was there for a week before I started recognizing who was there everyday. My room did pass inspection that next morning. I worked the entire evening removing everything from the room, cleaning everything before putting it back in its place. The lesson I learned was that without sufficient reason Colvert could not kick me out, and as long as I didn't quit, then I could stay. In fact, I never saw Colvert kick anybody out. But I did see a lot of people quit.

Saturdays were only slightly different from weekdays. We were up at 0500 spending three hours in intense cleaning before Colvert's inspection. After the inspection we changed into PT gear, rolling our swimming trunks up in a towel, did our pull-ups and ran to the pool.

We stayed in PT clothes lining up along the sides, putting the towels behind us. Colvert stepped out on the diving board. This was the vantage point from which he conducted the exercises, evaluating our progress. In my case progress was slight. But in the four days since my arrival, some progress was being made. I could do thirty-six push-ups non-stop, fifty good flutter kicks and forty sit-ups before finally tiring and falling behind. Colvert could tell the difference between exhaustion and cheating.

"You want to quit?" he would ask when he knew we were cheating. It was enough motivation to make me and most of the others hold them out straighter, or pick up the pace.

An hour and a half was all Colvert could take and ordered us to change into our swim suits.

WE'RE ALL MAD, YOU KNOW

Three minutes was all it took to be back at pool side. The air was warming up even though it was still late February, or maybe it was just the heat produced from our over-exerted muscles. Colvert chose four team captains to pick people for their teams and I was, of course, the last man chosen. We were swimming relay races with each man swimming fifty meters, five times. To my own amazement I found I could out-swim Carpenter, and he didn't like that very much. It did gain me some respect with the others and even Colvert nodded his head at me, which was praise indeed coming from him.

After the race we were ordered to swim underwater the length of the pool with one breath. The only time we had to rest was the amount of time it took for each member of our team to complete the distance before we would go back in again. On the last trip I must have surfaced five times, barely getting a breath before Colvert would yell, "Get under or get out!"

"Line up along the length of the pool," was our next command, followed by the command of "hit it." We dove into the pool and swam underwater to the other side, climbed out in a continuous leap, then turned around to get set again because "hit it" would sound seconds later. Twenty times we darted back and forth across the width of the pool. Toward the end my arms were so weak I crawled over the edge, stumbling to get turned around just as Colvert had yelled "hit it" again. By this time I was falling into the water instead of diving in and spent more time with my head above the water than under it. I wondered how every exercise he came up with could be harder than the last. But even this came to an end, and we swam circles around the pool for another thirty minutes before the base swim team arrived for their turn with the pool.

I prayed that we would go back to the barracks from there, but we couldn't be that lucky. We took a straight shot to the track for three miles of a pace my body was just now starting to get used to. Though I still could not join in the singing, I could stay with the team in tight formation.

The end of February finally came. Everything remained the same, only with eight less people. The inspections took just as long and we dropped just as many times, but Colvert now had more time to harass each one of us. Carpenter missed the cut off date to go with the senior class to Sheppard AFB for advanced training by only a few weeks, and that did not help his attitude any. There were ten of us now, which gave us plenty of room in the basement for the sadomasochistic rituals that took place down there. Probably the most amazing change that happened was that I was damn near keeping up. I even sang part of the time while we ran.

Tom McLafferty was the last man to join our team, getting in just before the cut off date. He was remarkable because this guy had no more business being there than I did. To encourage him along during PT, it was often said, "If McGuire can do it, you can do it." I wasn't sure if that made me feel good or not. We went that day for a flight physical that we had to pass to stay in, and everyone did. I asked the flight surgeon if he had some "horse linament" or something that I could soothe my aching muscles with. He gave me a whole case of some wintergreen smelling liquid for the whole team. From then on the entire barracks smelled of it. It went on feeling icy cold but soon began warming and got really hot. We were bathing in the stuff. Every so often, someone would run, screaming down the hall to the latrine to wash off after accidentally getting some on their testicles.

We left one morning on a run across base to fire the M-16 rifle. For the past couple of days I had been dragging worse than usual and was glad to have an "easy" day. The first hours of the morning were spent in a class room going over how the rifle works, how to load, aim and fire it. We were issued 110 rounds of ammunition and three empty clips and walked over to the target range. We loaded the clips and waited. I could see that the target was the silhouette of a man from the waist up, one hundred yards away.

"Ready on the left," the safety man called out, "ready on the right. Ready on the firing line. Ten rounds for sight adjustment. Commence firing."

I squeezed off ten rounds and we walked down to check the targets. My shots had hit low and to the right. We returned to the firing line, made sight adjustments and fired the remaining one hundred rounds into a fresh target. I blamed my sore throat and general ill feeling for a miss, and the fact that the pattern of holes were scattered widely across the target. After we finished the firing range we fell in for the run back to barracks singing as we ran.

We passed by the base hospital, and since I had been sick for a few days I asked Carpenter if I could go in and get looked at. I was chilled and my throat hurt each time

I swallowed but his reply was, "You're a bellyaching wimp McGuire. Either stay in step or quit."

I was in the lead with Carpenter, and each time we came to an intersection he would yell, "Road guards, post!" The two lead men would spring ahead to stop traffic, while the formation ran through, they would then fall in at the rear. We were both glad when my turn came because neither one of us liked running beside the other. He made me sing even though I sounded like a goat, but I stopped as soon as I was out of reach.

Back at the barracks that afternoon I was laying on my bunk knowing I had to shake this sore throat by 0500 or I would not last. Just then Carpenter opened the door. "Get your ass to the infirmary now, McGuire," he yelled, "and you better be one sick son-of-a-bitch."

I grabbed my baseball cap, did my pull-ups and ran the mile and a half to the open bay infirmary where the first thing they did was stick a thermometer in my mouth. To my complete relief it read 103.8. I asked to use the phone and called the barracks to report my condition. As the phone rang, I wondered if they could kick me out for being too sick to continue.

"They want to keep me here for a few days until I get over this," I said apologetically to Colvert when he answered the phone.

"You just rest and get your strength back," he said in a tone I hadn't heard from him before. "When you're well you just come on back."

After three days of down time and medication I arrived at the barracks feeling strong as I did my pull-ups and hustled up stairs to report back. Colvert didn't exactly

smile but he did say, "Welcome back." That was just before he told me to "drop!"
So much for liking sergeant Colvert.

Ed Setchfield had been training for three weeks before I moved in. He didn't have any use for me either at first, but had became more tolerant in the past few weeks. The developing camaraderie was evident in subtle forms occasionally showing through the hostility that lingered in the air. Setchfield was manning the front desk the Saturday night I tried to sneak a young WAF into the barracks.

I had met her a few hours earlier at the bowling alley. She seemed to be looking at me from across the crowded room and at first I thought, "surely not me." But after she returned my smile, I thought I should at least say hello.

"Is your beer hot?" I asked, noticing that she wasn't drinking it.

"No," she said. "I just don't like the guy that bought it for me. He said he was a PJ, but when I asked him if he knew you and he didn't, I knew he was lying. He left when he saw you coming."

"You recognized me?" I asked.

"I get to watch you guys sometimes. You're the one that's always bringing up the rear."

"That's me," I confessed.

We drank a few beers talking about where we were from and why the hell anyone would join the Air Force, before suggesting we put four more beers in her purse and drink them at "my place."

"All right McGuire," Setchfield said as we walked by the desk. We went into the day room to watch TV while we drank the beer and I was looking forward to wherever the evening might lead. Before we had time to get comfortable and open the first beer, Setchfield opened the door and warned in a soft voice, "A sky cop and his dog followed you up here. Use the back fire escape while I stall him." A "Sky Cop" is an Air Force security policeman, similar to an Army M.P.

He had denied seeing anyone come through so the cop started looking down the opposite end of the hall. When Setchfield closed the fire door between us and the cop, we ran down the hall to the emergency exit, climbed down the stairs and ran to make good our escape.

We didn't stop running until we fell behind some bushes several blocks away, looking back to be sure we weren't followed. We laughed until our sides ached and drank the now hot beer that foamed all over us when we opened them. With people milling around only a hundred feet away, the date became all that I had hoped for and then some.

After walking her back to her barracks, she kissed me on the cheek, looked me in the eye and smiled as she said, "Thank you."

I assured her she was quite welcome and asked when I might see her again. She shook her head, looked down at the ground and said, "You won't."

She turned and ran into her barracks. I never saw her again. I thanked Ed for saving my ass. He told me I could do the same for him some day.

Phil Parker, the next to the last man to join our team, was not nearly so lucky and got caught by the sky cops when he tried sneaking a WAF into the barracks. He was

32

not taken to jail but instead released to the custody of Colvert. The following day Parker had to stay in a leaning rest with his feet on a desk top for one hour. That was the one and only time an individual was punished instead of the entire team. From our rooms we could hear the agonizing moans and groans he was making, and that was after only forty minutes. Every so often we could hear Colvert demand that he sign the quit sheet. In true Pararescue style he refused. When his hour was completed he cradled his arms to his chest and walked to his room where he soaked his arms down with lineament. No one tried to sneak a female into the barracks after that.

One morning Kee told us that a PJ had been seriously injured in a helicopter crash in Vietnam. He was here at the base hospital and would be replacing Kee as soon as he recovered. It was two weeks later when we saw him for the first time.

His mouth was wired shut, and his bottom jaw had been reconstructed. He talked very little, but he did manage to tell us what had happened to him. He had been flying in a Jolly Green Giant rescue helicopter over the seaward end of the Mekong Delta when the aircraft suddenly came under intensive ground fire, taking hits all over the place.

The chopper was disabled to the point that it would no longer fly, and the crew knew they would be forced to ditch in the water. Fuel lines were ruptured and JP-4 jet fuel was running all over the interior of the helicopter. JP-4 does not mix well with salt water, and tends to form a very caustic solution that eats flesh.

33

WE'RE ALL MAD, YOU KNOW

Knowing this, the crew elected to attempt to jump out of the machine before it actually hit the water. The pilot "frictioned down" the controls so that the aircraft would continue downrange beyond the jump site, but his efforts did not work. A helicopter is inherently unstable, and as soon as the crew jumped out, the machine rolled to the right, then nosed down almost on top of the crewmembers who were by then floating in the water.

The tip on one of the main rotor blades hit the PJ squarely in the mouth, and his skin was severly burned with the fuel and salt water mixture that gushed out of the sinking fuselage.

It was a miracle he was still alive.

We seldom saw him, as he spent most of his time in the hospital. But seeing him confirmed just how dangerous this job could be. It didn't make any of us quit, but it made us think. If anything, it actually strengthened our resolve to continue.

I finally received a permanent roommate in the second week of March. His name was Geza Ludanie, a full blood Hungarian smuggled into the United States when he was a small boy. He still spoke with a pronounced accent and it was a pleasure listening to him talk. He had been two classes ahead of us, but had broken his arm while in jump school. Since he had already been through Sheppard, I asked him about what I could expect when I got there. But he had been ordered not to tell any of the secrets that awaited us there, and he refused to share any. I would have to find out for myself.

WE'RE ALL MAD, YOU KNOW

The last three days of that same week we caught a bus to Brooks Air Force Base, about ten miles away, for flight training. We were told on the last day we would spend several hours in the altitude chamber. The classroom instruction dealt with scanning techniques and spatial disorientation and as interesting as it was, we were even more happy to escape PT. The morning we were to go to the chamber was almost a disaster.

Geza, not having any clean-up duties, or required PT, turned my alarm clock off before it woke me up and my absence went unnoticed until the bus had already pulled away. Light coming through the window shining in my face woke me and I jumped out of bed in shock and disbelief. I ran to the office dressed only in my underwear.

"Can you drive me to Brooks?" I begged Kee's secretary, who thankfully was the only one there.

"I don't have a car," she replied as she reached for the phone. "I'll call you a taxi while you get dressed. You may just have time to make it." The clock was racing past 0735.

"Damn, damn, damn," was all I could say as I ran to my room and dressed. Today was payday, which meant I didn't have any money. Geza only had a five dollar bill. The secretary had a twenty saying, "Pay me back when you can."

I gave her the five, taking the twenty and ran down the stairs, doing 10 quick pull-ups, and looked around for my taxi. It hadn't arrived yet. My impatience made me feel the need to urinate but the sight of the taxi helped calm me down a little bit.

WE'RE ALL MAD, YOU KNOW

"What time is it?" I demanded to know as I jumped in the front seat. The driver was slow and methodical in telling me it was "not quite ten 'til" before starting off.

"You don't seem to understand," I told him when we got off the base, "just how much of a hurry I'm in."

"If I get pulled over you'll be late for sure," he replied and gave it a little more gas to make me feel better.

It was a few minutes after 0800 when we entered Brooks and "damn" was my entire vocabulary. "Damn, damn, damn!"

I directed him to the building we were training in from the edge of my seat, pleading for him to hurry every chance he got. The charge on the meter was around twelve dollars but it was 0812 by the time we arrived so I tossed him the twenty dollar bill and leaped from the taxi at a dead run before it even stopped rolling. I didn't wait for change.

I flew through the doors of the building and hauled ass down the long corridor toward the chamber. Captains and colonels alike were getting out of my way as it was obvious I wasn't stopping for anything. When I opened the door to the chamber room, to my complete astonishment, the last man on the team was stepping inside. I grabbed a mask hanging from the wall and slid through the concave airlock door as it was being closed by the safety man inside. I had made it with not one second to spare. I looked over at Carpenter as I took my seat, hooking up to the intercom and air supply, and tried to catch my breath. The look in his eyes told me I had just ruined his day.

A surgical glove had been tied at the wrist and hung from the chamber ceiling. We watched as the glove

36

expanded to several times its original size from the effect of sucking air out of the chamber. At a simulated altitude of forty thousand feet the glove was so large it looked as though it were about to burst.

Three controllers sat outside the chamber watching us through the glass, talking to us over the intercom.

"We need a volunteer for a demonstration," one of them said.

Reflex action sent my hand into the air first. The Safety Man handed me a small black box with a row of lights across the top and below each light was a small button.

"This is a simple demonstration of anoxia," the man outside said. "When a light comes on you are to press the button below it which will cause another light to come on whether you press the right button or not. Keep pressing buttons as long as you can. Do you understand?"

"Yes," I assured him, "I understand."

"Okay," he said, "take off your mask."

The first thing I noticed was the smell. As the pressure in the chamber decreased, the gasses in our bodies expanded and everyone 'passed gas.' The chamber reeked! A light on the box lit up immediately and it seemed childishly simple to push the button under it. The instant that light went out another light came on and I was pushing buttons as fast as I could for about ten seconds. Although I was breathing, there wasn't enough oxygen to support a flame, much less a life. The lights began to blur. I tried to focus my eyes but couldn't. My arm felt like rubber, unable to move it where I wanted it to go. I don't remember, but I was told later that at the end I was weaving back and forth and had hit three wrong buttons before the safety man put the oxygen mask back on my face.

I do remember him shaking me asking, "Are you all right?"

I was breathing deep and fast, feeling dizzy, but I told him, "Sure, I'm fine."

"Your hyperventilating," came the voice from outside, "control your breathing."

It took me five minutes to regaining my composure. The controller repeated what we had learned in class; to memorize the aircraft air exhaust ports and waste no time getting hooked up if rapid decompression occurs. If you hold your breath during rapid decompression, the expanding air in your lungs will rupture the alveoli like a bomb exploding (known as a pneumothorax), and if you breath to avoid the above you lose the oxygen keeping you alive.

We made a controlled "descent" as air was slowly put back in the chamber. I watched as the glove got smaller and smaller as the pressure outside the glove increased until we stopped at a simulated altitude of twenty five thousand feet. We were cautioned again to continue breathing normally and the chamber door was electronically opened creating a dull explosion. Instantly a thick layer of fog formed about a foot deep on the chamber floor, but dissipated rapidly.

The chamber was an interesting experience and on the bus back to the barracks I thought of how close I came to missing it--and for that matter being kicked out of Pararescue. Everyone, including Carpenter, agreed that there was no reason to say anything to Colvert about the incident. They also agreed that I was one of the luckiest people they had ever seen. Luck and determination were the only things I had on my side.

Geza didn't make a habit of turning off my alarm, but he did do it one more time causing me to miss an entire morning. Luckily, Colvert and Kee both failed to show up as well. Carpenter had quit waking me up after the first week and as busy as everyone was, it was easy to not notice if someone was missing.

"Come on," Geza said, "I'll work out and run with you so no one will have a reason to complain, and," he promised, "I won't turn off your alarm again." The team had finished their run and was on the way back to the barracks when Geza and I left the barracks headed for the track.

"You're in big trouble this time, McGuire!" Carpenter yelled as we ran by them in opposite directions.

"I'll explain when we get back," Geza yelled back to him, and the two of us ran the three miles together before going back to explain to Carpenter.

Geza's story satisfied Carpenter and everyone else except for Steve Hutchinson, who said he was going to tell Colvert the next morning. Hutchinson was one of those guys who truly belonged in Pararescue. He was an Olympic quality athlete who felt I didn't belong there. No matter how we tried, he could not be talked out of it. I worried about it the whole night and all the way through the inspection. When we met downstairs for PT he was suspiciously absent. But he wasn't snitching to Colvert because somebody had locked him in his locker. Now he too was guilty of missing a workout, so how could he tell on me?

That was the first time I really felt accepted, and completed the session feeling stronger than I ever felt before.

Running around a track is boring as well as strenuous, and Carpenter finally got permission from Kee to let us run around the back streets of the base to give us some new scenery to look at. We explored in different directions for the first few days, not caring how far we ran. We hit pay dirt on the day we discovered where the WAF drill field was and made sure we passed that way every day. That is until the day we were confined to the track again. It was not the compliments we made about their legs that pissed off the WAF Commander, but rather the obscenities in our songs. We missed their smiles and the rare occasion when one of them would lift their skirt a little to show some leg.

We were joined late one night by six guys from two classes ahead of us. The sound of counting coming from outside woke me up. When I opened my door, Carpenter and everyone else was already in the hall.

"Get back to bed," he half whispered, "this has nothing to do with us, and I don't want it to."

During PT the following morning, we got an explanation. The people whose voices we heard had just completed Jump School, but their SCUBA school wasn't starting for another week. They were forced to return here.

Not expecting Colvert to be waiting for them, they bloused their dress blues--something we weren't allowed to do until we graduated from transition school. Colvert could have kicked them all out for this transgression. He didn't, but he made them pay.

The only thing we found out from them when we had a chance to talk was that "You had better get tougher than you are now, or you'll never make it."

We didn't like the sound of that.

The month of March lasted so long I was beginning to think it would never end. But Friday, March 31st did finally come around and after inspection, Carpenter called us all into the day room before going outside for PT. (We stopped going to the basement as soon as the weather warmed up enough to reduce the risk of pneumonia.)

"I just left Colvert's office and he asked us to do him a favor. He has a bar off base and business is not so good, so he said that if all of us would go out to his bar tonight to help fill the place up, that he would buy us all a beer and tomorrow morning there will be no inspection or PT."

We all whooped and hollered and started jumping up and down at the thought of having a whole weekend off for getting drunk. It seemed too good to be true, but no one suspected for a minute that it might be a trap.

Carpenter lead us through the toughest PT we had ever done saying we had to make up for tomorrow's PT that we were going to sleep through. It was so hard that two new boys that were beginning the next class almost quit. We only did one eight-count "body builder" that lasted for fifteen minutes by itself because Carpenter kept going from "seven" back to "one" or any number in between, avoiding number eight until he could do it no longer. I was stumbling all over myself trying to keep up. When we finished our pull-ups after the run we buried ourselves in our rooms to recuperate. No one went to the laundry to pick up or drop off fatigues. We didn't have our boots shined, or do anything else to prepare for Saturday. Why bother?

That evening we left the barracks doing our pull-ups, but instead of running in formation we walked at our leisure out the main gate and down the road about a mile to Colvert's bar. It was a real "hole-in-the-wall," but we had a good drunk just the same. That is, up until the moment Carpenter poured some beer on my head. I had been sitting alone in a booth with a beer in my hand, watching two girls dancing. I didn't see him coming as he sat down across from me.

"What's it going to take to get rid of you, McGuire?" a mean, drunk Carpenter asked.

"You've gotta do better than you're doing now," I answered, drunk and feeling cocky.

With a smile on his face he leaned forward and poured the beer over my head. I just sat there and let him do it. When he sat back and gave me that "what are you going to do about it" look, I poured some beer over his head.

"Let's go out back and talk about this," Carpenter offered.

I must have been really drunk, because at that moment I thought I was his equal. "Let's go," I said.

We no more than got outside, when he turned and cold-cocked me.

I squared off to defend myself. Carpenter took a step back with his fists raised. "Come on McGuire," he said. "I've been looking forward to this."

I believed him. I also instantly realized I was no match for him. I lowered my guard and said, "I can't take you."

"No you can't," he said matter-of-factly, and walked back inside.

I was drunk enough not to feel any pain and rejoined the team. Carpenter ignored me except for any opportunity to be an ass. There was open hatred between us. Carpenter had received a ration of shit from Colvert for allowing me to drop out early on that run during my first day of training and held it against me ever since. I appreciated what he did for me then, but he was easy to hate now.

We drank up our taxi money and had to walk back, stumbling and crawling as best we could do. Several stops were required to heave our guts up.

The bell on the phone in Colvert's office rang loud Saturday morning. I could hear it from my room. My alarm clock said 0745, so I pulled the pillow over my head to muffle the sound. I heard Carpenter's door open on about the fifteenth ring, and three rings later he answered it. During the short pause that followed I thought of how good it felt to lay in bed, but that was short lived. Carpenter hung up the phone and in a panic stricken scream said, "The son-of-a-bitch is going to be here in ten minutes!"

It was Saturday, April the First, and a bigger group of April fools had never been assembled. Sergeant Colvert had set us up, and in ten minutes he was going to knock us down.

Everyone scrambled out of bed and met in the hall wishing it was just a bad dream. The look on Carpenter's face told us this was real.

"I don't have any clean fatigues!" McLafferty said followed by a chorus of, "My boots aren't shined," and "What the hell are we going to do now?"

"All right, all right. Hold it down," Carpenter called out after having a moment to think. "We're all in this together so everybody wears dirty fatigues. We have about five minutes, so get dressed, keep your mouths shut and just take whatever comes."

We were all scared shitless when we heard the door close downstairs, but there wasn't time to go to the latrine now. Colvert intentionally stomped his boots on each rung as he slowly ascended the stairs, stopping in the doorway that entered the hall to our rooms. He stood there for a long time, savoring the moment. His immaculate uniform could not cover the look on his face that showed us he hadn't had very much sleep. His initial look of satisfaction at having been successful at catching us unprepared changed to complete disgust at the sight he was looking at. It felt like the guillotine was about to fall.

Slowly he walked up to Carpenter's face, towering a few inches above him, and barked, "You're a disgrace Carpenter! You're supposed to be the class leader! Well, I wouldn't let you lead my pig to slop. You're fired as class leader Carpenter! Drop!"

Military precision demands that you move without hesitation, so we all dropped and knocked out push-ups like a chorus line. He let us recover after each set, but never took his eyes off of us. While we were doing push-ups, he walked up and down the center of the hall, looking back every so often to make sure no one cheated.

Steve Birkland was as big and friendly as any man you will ever meet. Six foot two and an easy three hundred pounds. We called him the Jolly Green Giant. He labored harder at PT than anyone to keep his bulk in cadence, producing the strength you would expect from a giant. He lived across the hall from Carpenter, and was next to face Colvert. Colvert may have had to look up at him, but he was not intimidated.

"You're the new class leader, Birkland!" Colvert barked as he marched into Birkland's room. A few seconds passed when we heard a short burst of obscenities followed by a thunderous, "You're fired, Birkland. Drop!" He repeated this sequence with the next four men he came to--Prado, Parker, Hutchinson, and Ray MacMahon--saying the rest of us were not worthy of consideration. He was getting meaner with each man he came to. He even grabbed Mike Dunlap by the collar and threw him into his room, then followed him in. Dunlap was a quiet, shy man who never gave Colvert reason to be angry before. But today, Colvert was pissed at everybody.

"I'll see to it that you never become a PJ!" he yelled from there. We dropped again. Every few seconds Colvert would lean over someone and scream his lungs out to sign "the paper" and get out of his life.

My turn was drawing near, but not soon enough. I was getting weaker by the minute. We moaned, groaned, quivered, shook, and were dripping sweat. I just had to cheat. When his back was turned, I let my belly rest on the floor, relieving the weight from my quivering arms. I was watching Colvert so closely that I could sense him turning around, and was off the ground in time. It was dangerous, but even Carpenter laid down once just to spite him.

He was standing directly over me when we recovered, which put him in my face as I stood at attention. He glared at me through bloodshot eyes that got larger while the veins in his neck stood out. The muscles in his cheeks were twitching. I thought he was going to jump on me with both feet but instead he spit right in my face.

"I hate your guts, McGuire!" he screamed immediately afterwards.

My sleeve was moving to wipe the spit from my face when he yelled, "You're at attention airman. You should've been out of here a long time ago, but I doubt you will last the rest of this day. Drop!"

I had enough rest from the last set and enough adrenaline from him spitting on me that I nearly made thirty-six nonstop. Colvert insisted I continue before I had time to shake out my first arm, so after two more I was spreading my legs apart, almost touching the floor with my pelvis and rocking back and forth in an effort to get my body off the ground. I stopped in the leaning rest unable to do one more, even with Colvert threatening to kick me out. One at a time I finished the set squirming for each one.

"Recover," he said when I was done, stepping across the hall at the same time. Setchfield was just getting to his feet as Colvert knocked him up against the wall screaming, "Get out of my space!"

WE'RE ALL MAD, YOU KNOW

The atmosphere was scary to say the least, and had we been on the high seas his violence would have driven us to mutiny. There was nothing we could do here but take it. Three more times we dropped before the inspection was over. He re-hired Carpenter as class leader as he walked by him, telling him to have us ready for PT at the pool in fifteen minutes. When Colvert was out of earshot, we cursed his mother with every breath we took.

Colvert was standing on the diving board as we ran up to take our positions at pool-side. "Do twice the number of exercises that you normally do," he ordered from his perch.

For the next twenty-five minutes we did side-straddle-hops, "cherry-pickers" and "squat thrusts." The number was one hundred four-count repetitions of each. The insides of my thighs were knotting up and cramping, but I was thankful for the delay of the really hard exercises to come. Half way through the "windmills" he waved his arms screaming, "Enough of this bullshit. I want to see some push-ups!"

Carpenter hesitated for a second before ordering seventy, four-count push-ups. The hypnotic effect of our rhythmic counting was getting to Colvert, who sat down on the board and told us during one of our stops to run eight miles after PT. He finally laid down on the board and appeared as if he had passed clean out.

We kept right on knocking out pushups as if he were standing over us. Seventy, plus one for Pararescue, arrived leaving us too weak to stand. Kneeling in the fetal position was as close as any of us could come to recovering and

WE'RE ALL MAD, YOU KNOW

Carpenter asked very softly, "What do you want to see next?"

When he didn't get a response, he and Birkland walked over to Colvert cautiously and shook him a little. But Colvert was out like a light. It was just as well because the swim team was waiting to use the pool. Six guys lifted him to their shoulders, and much like pallbearers, carried him to the barracks as we ran in formation singing in a whisper how much we liked it here. He was taken up stairs and put to bed before we fell back in to run to the track.

For the first three miles we sang and laughed about how we got out of doing flutter kicks and all of the pool work. We still had five miles to go. The pace was unrelenting and the third wind had taken control, turning us into machines with only one purpose; to run. Cross country is one thing but marathon is quite another. We were getting tired of repeating the same songs, so Carpenter made some up as he went along. Still, we had two miles to go.

I started noticing a sharp pain in the front of my lower legs along the length of the tibia. I was developing shin splints, or tiny stress fractures, that only rest can cure.

But there was precious little of that.

I was able to endure by some inner strength that everyone possesses, but few ever get to experience. After seven and a half miles, some fifty minutes, McLafferty asked the question that we all wanted an answer to. "How in the hell is that son-of-a-bitch going to know if we stop short of eight miles?"

"He's not going to know," was Carpenter's reply, and on the next pass he lead us back to the barracks. We did our pull-ups and went upstairs to find Colvert was gone.

WE'RE ALL MAD, YOU KNOW

We had all survived, but not without wounds. Both to our bodies and minds.

But there was no way anyone would quit now. There became a favorite saying around the barracks when someone would ask where someone else was. We would say, "I think he quit."

We didn't lounge around that weekend but instead had your basic "GI party" to the Pararescue extreme. The following Monday morning we were inspection-ready when both sergeants Kee and Colvert searched everywhere looking for dust. That morning we only dropped once per man, which was a sign we were reaching our goal.

We looked like the old class that was here when I first arrived forty-five days before, being able to perform with the precision of a machine.

On Friday, April the 7th, we were measured for the wetsuit that was tailored-made by White Stag, which would be issued to us at Hill AFB, Utah, should we get that far. Colvert did the measuring, harassing me on how skinny I was.

He had one other thing for us: our orders.

We each got a large manila envelope containing close to one hundred copies. We sat silent and stunned there in the day room. This was a day we never thought we would see. We lived in constant fear of not being here the next day, much less graduate. We were no longer the lowest form of life on earth, we were entering the pipeline of PJ training.

"When are we leaving?" Setchfield finally asked.

WE'RE ALL MAD, YOU KNOW

"Stand by," Colvert ordered as we started opening the envelopes. "You're not out of here yet. Everybody you meet is going to want a copy of those, so don't lose them. All right, you can open them now."

The orders were a page and a half of military jargon saying briefly that we had a Secret security clearance and listed the itinerary of dates and locations of the various schools we were to attend. It was an overwhelming relief to receive them--especially when we read the departure date. We would be leaving for Shepherd on April 12, 1972...only five days away!

After Saturday's workout we went to a park off base for a going-away party. Incredibly, the bill was paid by Kee and Colvert. We ate a picnic lunch and drank enough beer to get loose, but not enough to get rowdy. The next few days dragged by with Carpenter not letting up on the PT but taking it a little lighter on us.

The morning we were to leave finally came around.

We put just as much effort into our clean-up details as we ever did and Colvert put just as much effort into making us quit as he ever did. We thought the day before that we were doing our last PT, but like so many times before we were wrong again. This PT was easy as Carpenter felt we had paid our dues. Maybe it just seemed easy because we were in shape and we knew this had to be the last time we busted our asses around here.

We sang loud during the run, laughing at things that weren't funny at the time and being more vulgar in our description of the "legs" along side of the road than we ever dared before. The last lap felt so good we whooped and hollered and jumped up and down completely out of step, going absolutely mad with elation after finishing the pull-ups.

It really was over.

All we had left to do now was to eat, pack our bags and wait for the bus. Our next stop would be Sheppard Air Force Base, the first real taste of Pararescue training. Our questions regarding "the secrets" were about to be answered.

Chapter Three

Sheppard

Except for the dress blues we were wearing, everything we owned was contained in two duffel bags. It wasn't until 2330 that we left the barracks for the last time. The occasion was somber as each of us did our last "ten" on the pull-up bar plus the infamous "one for Pararescue."

We waited at the same corner where I had been deposited by the bus fifty-eight days ago, thinking that if I knew then what I know now, I probably would go through it again. This moment felt that good.

The headlights coming toward us were too close together to be a bus. In fact, it was Colvert. We all stood quiet as he pulled over and got out of his car. After looking at us for a moment in the fashion that he always did, he walked over to the trunk of the car, opened it, and pulled out a case of beer.

"Just wanted to see you men off," he said.

We screamed "hoo yah!" and "blood and guts!" all together while trotting over to grab a can of beer. While we drank, he gave us a little speech:

."and some of you," he said looking at me, "I wouldn't have given a snowball's chance in hell of getting this far. I'm proud of every one of you. There's no reason why all of you shouldn't become PJ's. Sergeant Wilson is waiting for you at Sheppard, but I believe you're ready for him. Maybe I'll see you again sometime." He then gave us the first smile I had seen since the briefing in basic.

We guzzled down the remaining beer as the bus pulled up. Colvert leaned up against his car while we stowed our bags in the outside compartment and boarded the bus. He watched until the bus rolled away and out of sight. I never saw sergeant Colvert again.

We changed buses at a depot on base, boarding with other GIs headed for Sheppard. They too were wearing dress blues with the "bus driver" style hat, so to be different we changed to the aviator's cap. It was 0200 before we got off base, and sleep came easy.

When we woke up at the first stop that morning it was daylight. Everyone got out to stretch their legs and get a bite to eat. None of us had anything to say, and we must have appeared arrogant to the others. But they couldn't know the apprehension gnawing in our guts. About a half hour out from Sheppard the gnawing began to burn as my imagination only got worse. How often we were told, that if you make it through Sheppard then you'll make it through Pararescue. Since this place was going to be the worst of it, then we had good reason to worry.

It was early afternoon when the bus turned into Sheppard AFB just outside of Wichita Falls, Texas. The other GIs on the bus were laughing and talking loud while my team sat in complete silence, scared shitless until McLafferty pointed out in the distance saying, "There's the pool."

My gut rolled again as I looked at the large bubble dome that housed a giant pool. After several stop lights and turns we rounded a corner that lead to the depot. Standing on the dock was sergeant Wilson, the beret making him easy to spot. Beside him was an airman with bloused fatigues and a blue dickey. Our eyes were glued on them as we pulled to a stop.

A real team will unconsciously do the same thing at the same time as if it were only one person doing the thinking. We were a "real team" because we would be acting just that way many times during the next month, starting right now.

The ten of us sat completely motionless as all the other GIs stood to collect their carry on baggage. Wilson moved in confident strides in front of the bus and sprang up the steps. "Sit down, you legs!" he screamed in a tone we were used to, but the others weren't. The Air Force is not known for its high degree of military discipline. They weren't moving fast enough so Wilson yelled again, "Sit down!"

This time they fell into their seats.

WE'RE ALL MAD, YOU KNOW

"If any of you think you have what it takes to be a PJ, then get your ass off this bus." We jumped up immediately and began moving for the door.

"Get your duffel bags and line them neatly on the grass!" he ordered before half of us were off the bus. "Move your asses! I've waited on you pissants all that I'm going to."

We piled our bags and fell in a arms-length interval, standing at attention.

"Drop!" he yelled a second later, coming as no surprise. Thirty-six pushups came easy, but so did the sweat. A record-breaking heat wave had just started that would last a week.

"I told you slobs to line those bags up neatly," Wilson roared. "Recover and straighten them up!"

We lined them up and fell back in just in time to be told to "drop" again. The GIs on the bus were still in their seats, watching us through the windows. Wilson let them get off during the third set. We started getting out of sequence toward the end, and I had to rest once before finishing. When we recovered, our dress blue shirts were soaked with sweat, as was our hair and faces.

"Anybody want to quit?" Wilson asked, as if someone really would. "Then lets see how tough you guys really are. Drop!"

He paced in front of our faces watching us writhe in pain and sweat. Carpenter called for a leaning rest at thirty, which if he had not I was going to anyway. After shaking them out and wiping the sweat out of our eyes, we knocked out the remaining five plus one for Pararescue.

"Recover and throw your bags in the back of the truck," Wilson ordered. We jumped up yelling "blood and guts," did what we were told and fell in behind the truck in two columns. We ran along behind the truck to the barracks, a distance of well over a mile, singing as we went.

Our barracks stood alone on a large patch of ground with a dirt path circling the perimeter of the grounds. No sooner had we come to a halt than Wilson got right back on our case.

"You all look like a bunch of ducks," he said, belittling each of us. "So walk and talk like ducks. Twice around the path, move!"

Duck walking is squatting at the knees, waddling one leg in front of the other and quacking. It was nearly a quarter of a mile around the path and the dust we were kicking up stuck to our sweaty dress blues and we were spitting mud out of our throats.

"Pick it up," Wilson screamed each time we tried to slow down. This was a new experience in pain. The back of my calves burned, as did my thighs and lungs. Half way through the second lap we hurt so badly that our quacks sounded more like cries. I just couldn't take it any more and fell to my knees to crawl for a while to ease the pain.

"Get up!" I heard Wilson yell as soon as my knees hit the ground. That instant of relief enabled me to travel another twenty yards before the pain was unbearable again. This time I raised up a little but it didn't help much. I was getting dizzy from heat exhaustion, and the loss of so much body fluid from sweating so hard. Still the precious liquid leaked from our pores. Unconsciousness would have been a blessing. When we crossed the line where we started, everybody fell to their hands and knees, out of breath as any wrestler after a hard match. Sergeant Wilson really didn't care.

"Fall in!" he ordered, not giving us but five seconds to catch our breath. We jumped up screaming "hoo yah" the best we could while lining up at attention.

"Drop!" he yelled as soon as we were ready and fell to the ground again. We completed the set thinking he was trying to kill us but as we were recovering he explained to us what grass drills were and then we knew he was trying to kill us. "On your back! On your feet! On your stomach! On your feet! On your back!" he commanded as fast as he could.

We followed his commands for the first thirty seconds or so before we started lagging behind and flopping around like a group of epileptics in a grand mal seizure. When he called for attention we were barely able to stand, but it didn't matter because he said "drop" anyway. As tough as we were, he knew we were past the point of endurance and turned the water hose on us.

"Me! me!" we were pleading as we quivered in the leaning rest. The cool water drenching us gave us enough life to finish those thirty-six push-ups.

We had survived another onslaught of humiliating torture standing at attention after recovering in what was once our dress blues, still wearing ties.

"You guys are a mess," Wilson said, laughing at us. "Get this mess cleaned up and have that barracks inspection ready by 0800 tomorrow morning. Get your gear out of the truck and do your pull-ups. Hustle it up!"

WE'RE ALL MAD, YOU KNOW

The pull-up bar was eight feet off the ground and thirty feet long with support post at each end and two more spaced in between. The steel pipe was too big in diameter to grip, so our palms had to rest on the top of the bar with our fingers reaching as far as we could stretch them. For Setchfield, just getting up there was a major feat. By gripping a support bar in one hand he had to jump up and pull with all his might. Carpenter lead the count with all of us doing not ten, but fifteen pull-ups in unison, dropping to the ground at the same time.

Again we were in a two-story, WWII vintage barracks, only this one had obviously not been lived in for a while. Dust had settled everywhere and the barracks was anything but inspection ready when we went to bed at 2130. We occupied both the upstairs and downstairs rooms allowing each of us to have our own room.

At 0500 we were out of bed to continue the job that we started the night before to get ready for inspection. By 0745 we still weren't ready, but time had run out. At 0800 we were outside standing at attention when Wilson arrived. He spent a few moments getting a good look at each of us saying our name out loud as he came to us in an effort to remember each man.

"When you find some time I want you to have these fatigues tailored," he told us and went inside alone to do his inspecting. After a few minutes we heard him holler through the window, "This place is a sorry mess, drop!"

We might as well be at Lackland, I thought as we dropped and recovered for forty-five minutes. When he came back outside his attitude was a little more subdued. "Your classroom studies don't start until Wednesday of

WE'RE ALL MAD, YOU KNOW

next week. Between now and then you will be doing PT, and in your spare time this barracks better get spotless. You have one hour of free time starting now so be back, ready to go to the pool with your jock strap, trunks and two towels. Dismissed!"

The hour was over in a hurry and Wilson returned with several boxes of large, heavy swim fins, mask and snorkels for us to pick through to find a pair that fit. He watched us do our pull-ups, making sure that our arms extended fully with each down move and that our chins went above the bar on the up move. Fifteen plus one for Pararescue on a bar too big to grip was a formidable task. We collected our gear and ran to the pool, following Wilson who rode comfortably in a truck.

It was a few minutes after 1000 hours when we lined up along the length of the pool, wearing only our swim suites. The rest of our gear was lined up behind us. The pool was Olympic in size, fifty meters long (165 feet), and wide enough for all ten of us to have our own lane. From where we stood it looked scary. The numbers along the side of the pool said it was fourteen feet deep under the two diving boards, one low and one high. Wilson came in and stood by the high board. "All right Carpenter," he said, "warm 'em up."

We did our warm-up, sit-ups and push-ups in the same manner we were all use to except the repetitions were increased. That we could live with but no one was ready for what happened next.

"Get your fins on," Wilson ordered with a gleam in his eye. "Lay down with your butts on the edge of the pool and extend your legs out over the water. With each stroke

59

I want you to dip the fin under the water and throw the water as high as you can with each upstroke. Get ready."
We positioned our fists under our butts and raised our fin laden legs six inches above the water.

"Two hundred four-count flutter kicks. Ready, exercise!"

"Hot damn this is going to hurt," I murmured as all of us looked at each other in horror.

Starting with our left fin first, it went up dry as we lowered the right fin into the water on the count of one. As the right fin started up and I felt the suction that had to be overcome just to get it out of the water, I knew this was going to be the toughest thing we had done yet. I threw the water up at the height of the kick, counting "two." The left fin plopped into the water at the same time, and it too came out with considerable effort and unloaded at the top, counting "three" before repeating with the right leg again. That was only the first repetition. There were one hundred ninety-nine more to go.

"If you make it through Sheppard...." I remembered being told again. This was going to tell the story. At the hundredth repetition I couldn't believe we were only half way through. The third wind seemed to come over me like a wave, numbing the pain and disassociating my consciousness from my body. The effect didn't last long enough though, and by one-hundred-fifty the pain had returned. I was using my fist and rocking my body from side to side to help push my legs into the air.

"You're looking kind of sloppy," Wilson taunted. "Anybody want to quit?"

Hell yes, I wanted to quit. But we were too near the end now and "one-seventy-five" was coming up. In sheer desperation we kept our legs moving as the sound of our cadence grew louder. Groans of agony filled the air. By one-hundred-ninety-nine we were all screaming in an effort to release enough adrenaline to do two more, and we were at the top of our lungs when we exploded with one for Pararescue.

"Recover," Wilson ordered.

We screamed "hoo yah!" and "blood and guts!" as we scrambled to our feet coming to a sloppy attention, but we were standing. I prayed that this was the worst of it. I was wrong.

"Get your towels and go to the shallow end," Wilson ordered. We had been wondering what the towels were for since he told us to bring them, and now our curiosity was about to be satisfied. On command we stepped into the four foot deep water and listened as he explained what to do with the towels.

"Hold any corner with the thumb and index finger and lay that corner across the open palm of the other hand. Now make a fist so the towel doesn't fall out of your hand. You will note that some of the towel extends from both sides of your fist. That is wrong. Pull on the long end until the corner of the towel is even with the edge of your fist so that your little finger can still grip it but nothing shows beyond it. Now put the other towel in the other hand the same way."

He walked down the width of the pool checking each one of us in our lane for excess towel extrusion. "You are to swim to the other end, turn around and come back and

61

I want to see those towels come out of the water and hear it pop when you whip it forward."

His explanation was understood but somewhat farfetched as we soon discovered on the way down. Besides the weight of a towel full of water weighing us down, it also created a lot of drag making each stroke a battle of alternating between push and pull with very little forward progress. I wasn't the only one not popping my towels, but mine weren't even coming out of the water, doing what I thought was real good just to keep my head above water with ten meters to go before I could even turn around. On the way back I learned the valuable lesson in life to "pace thyself" and stopped fighting the towels. I discovered that when a towel went as far forward as I could throw it, I would put the other towel close to my body and lunge forward using the leading towel as an anchor. The momentum obtained was slight, but at least it was forward. The first time my big toe touched the bottom as we approached the shallow end was an accident, but after that it was on purpose. We finished within fifteen seconds of each other.

I knew this was not going to be my favorite exercise when, after maybe a minute, Wilson ordered "down and back." Half way down the realization that I might drown here this morning suddenly hit me. We were doing unrealistic numbers of repetitions of everything else so why should this be any different. On the way back my system began to fail me because I couldn't drag the trailing towel far enough forward.

"Oh God, this hurts," I told myself, resorting to a modified breast stroke that more closely resembled the panicked flailing of a drowning man than any bona fide swim stroke. This was hurting the strongest swimmer, and killing the rest of us.

"Down and back." Wilson ordered again. The "hoo yahs" and "blood and guts" we always yelled before each exercise showed less and less enthusiasm as we plunged forward. This was rapidly becoming the hardest thing we had ever done. I was unable to keep my face in the water more than five strokes after leaving toe-deep water because I was so short of breath. A wave swamped my face just as I turned and sucked in, only this time the bottom was fourteen feet deep. I coughed a couple of times, choking, and let panic overcome me. I blurted out, "I can't."

The instant I said it, the panic subsided from the realization that I had just quit. But since I hadn't dropped my towels, I kept swimming.

"Who said 'I can't' in there?" Wilson yelled, looking in my direction.

I didn't own up to it because I truly believed he would kick me out.

"Somebody better tell me who said that!" he screamed out at us.

No one said a word.

I was resting at the end while waiting for the last man to finish. Wilson stood directly over me.

"Did you say 'I can't' out there?" he asked me directly.

"No sergeant," I lied in response.

The last man just reached the end when Wilson said, "Well, we'll see 'who can't.' Down and back!"

"Who we are," I screamed out loud, plunging in head first. I wasn't going to quit. Using the bottom as long as I could and pacing myself, I was able to keep my burning shoulders and lungs turning and breathing.

True to form, the extremes of Pararescue were unrelenting. Wilson not only sent us down and back again but he was the proverbial broken record. He sent us down and back nine times.

When he said down and back for the tenth time, no one moved a muscle. The silence was eerie as we stood there, the whole team, starring at him. Wilson didn't find it amusing and seemed to grow in stature as the veins in his neck dilated and the look in his eyes said he could murder us all here and now.

"I said down and back!" he screamed with all the might he could muster and was met with a roar of "blood and guts" from us as we made our way on what finally ended up being the last trip.

We threw the towels over the edge of the pool and let our bodies drift in the weightless cool water that helped conduct the heat from our muscles. Wilson didn't let us enjoy it very long before he calmly told us, "Get your mask and fins and go to the deep end."

We didn't wear them during the towel swim, which I thought at first was too bad for us, until we sat along the edge of the deep end putting them on. We noticed, for the first time, several small and a couple of large areas on our feet that didn't have any skin. Sharp pain shot through me when each raw area came in contact with the fin.

"You better take a deep breath of air," Wilson suggested. "Fifty meters underwater with one breath. You have one minute to psyche yourselves up. Get in."

I started hyperventilating the instant I looked down the distance of fifty meters.

"Get ready," Wilson warned us. "*Go!*"

I thought for the first few meters that I was going to pass out. That happens when you hyperventilate then hold your breath, but the feeling passed and for the next few meters I felt pretty good. I watched the bottom as it rose gradually, convincing myself that I really didn't need to breathe. I practiced different strokes to discover which one gave me the most speed with the least effort. It seemed that a steady wide flutter kick, while alternating my arms forward and 'S'ing back close to my body slowly produced the least drag. The urge to breath was getting harder to resist and the far wall wasn't even close. I gutted it out for another ten meters, but the wall still wasn't visible. I surfaced when my intercostal muscles started involuntarily contracting so hard that I was sucking the mask to my face.

I was the third one up and still fifteen meters from the end. Within ten seconds everyone was above water except for Hutchinson, who made it to the end, surfacing last.

"You've got until Wednesday to reach the end or you're out!" Wilson told us bluntly. "Get out, get your towels and get dressed."

I glanced at the clock as we exited the air lock doors that held in the air pressure that kept the bubble dome over the pool inflated. My surprise was not that we were there for two solid hours but rather it had only been two hours. We hurt from the blisters on our feet to the aching in our shoulders, but nothing compared to putting on our shoes and socks. Wilson came into the locker room and grabbed

Carpenters mask, filling it with water from the fountain before handing it back to him.

"Put it on, Carpenter," he said, "and don't spill any."

We couldn't help but laugh, but Wilson immediately ordered us to do the same thing. "Anybody with less than a half mask full of water when you get to the barracks owes me one hundred push-ups." We fell in for the run back to the barracks.

"Miserable" is the only word to describe how we felt as we ran along carrying two wet towels, two heavy fins, the snorkel we didn't use, a mask full of water on our face, all the while singing and trying to see where we were going.

We must have been a pitiful sight because all activity stopped for fifty yards in either direction as we ran by. Cars pulled over to the side and people quit talking to stare at us. Wilson was waiting for us to do his mask inspection. Sure enough, two people had less than half full masks and were ordered to report to his office later to pay their debt.

After chow we had a couple of hours to spare. We used them by taking care of laundry and getting a month's supply of "mole skin" bandages from Carpenter to protect the open wounds on our feet. By 1900 we were at the track for night PT.

"So you guys think you're tough because you survived a sissy work-out at the pool," said Wilson. "Lets see if you can run!"

He lined us up on the goal line of the football field with the quarter mile track around it and bleachers along one side. "You have thirteen seconds to get to the other end," he informed us. "GO!"

WE'RE ALL MAD, YOU KNOW

Thirteen seconds is about how long it took, and that's about how long he gave us to rest before sending us back again. I fully expected to do this a few times, but on the thirteenth trip I wondered just when he was going to stop. My lungs burned with every breath and the pain in my sides wouldn't let me stand up. The thirteen second time limit was a joke from the fourth sprint and saliva dripped from our gaping mouths as we were unable to stop panting long enough to swallow. The last few sprints we didn't have the breath for a "hoo yah" but we did groan loud enough to at least make some kind of noise. It took us at least thirty seconds to finish number twenty with our legs wobbling like a new-born colt walking for the first time. The towel swim still ranks #1, but this was close.

For the next hour we did every exercise we knew how to do with a slight variation in the push-ups. We were simply to do as many as we could non-stop. Rick Prado was our champion doing sixty four and I mean perfect push-ups, lightly touching his chest to the ground and fully extending his arms. I did forty six. Small groups passing by would stop and watch from the stands, but soon became bored and went on.

We fell in on the track for what I was hoping was the run home since the sun had set and it would be dark soon. But no. Wilson ordered three miles around the track. The events of the day were wearing on us so Carpenter slowed the pace by a few seconds per lap. It was enough for Wilson to notice and he told us to pick it up a little. I noticed he had a stop watch on the next lap, and was nodding his head as we ran by saying, "That's better." It was pitch dark when we finished the last lap, but instead of coming to a halt, Wilson told us to head for the barracks.

We didn't believe Wilson was anywhere around, but we did our pull-ups anyway since the only time we cheated was when exhaustion prevented us from playing fair, and even then when we knew we wouldn't get caught. I tried to get undressed for a shower, but the socks wouldn't come off of my feet. They were stuck to seeping wounds on my skin. When I entered the shower, the team was there peeling their socks off under the hot water.

We compared blisters to see who's was the biggest and deepest. I think it was a tie between us all. I was asleep the instant my head hit the pillow.

Monday morning we felt a little better after having a half day to recuperate, but we were dragging our asses by day's end. Tuesday we were dragging before the inspection was over and were relieved to hear that Wilson had volunteered us to clean our classroom that evening instead of doing PT. Everyone finished the fifty meter underwater swim that morning a day ahead of the deadline, and threw water during the flutter kicks well past number one hundred before getting sloppy. Wilson continually asked us if we wanted to quit but having survived the first day we weren't about to quit now.

The sun had set as we ran toward our classroom, but it was still light enough to see a flight of GIs practicing close order drills ahead in the distance. Their drill instructor intentionally turned them on a head on collision course with us in a childish game of chicken.

"Pick it up a little," Carpenter said quietly as the distance between the forty of them and the ten of us was closing rapidly. He loved a good fight, and although he didn't change course to run into them, he didn't change course to avoid them either.

Carpenter was the first to burst into their ranks throwing fists and elbows at the ones that didn't jump out of the way before our momentum carried us into their midst.

"Halt!" Carpenter ordered, as GIs scattered from his reach. As out-numbered as we were the fight stopped before it got started. The drill instructor accused Carpenter of not yielding to his flight. "How about I just whip your ass, Sarge?" was his arrogant reply.

"You're lucky I don't bring charges against you," the sergeant answered back.

Carpenter just laughed at him. That seemed to end the argument as the old sarge had nothing else to say. Both groups reformed and we continued the run toward our classroom.

We arrived a few minutes late to find our instructor obviously pissed. "We got lost" were the only words spoken on the subject. For the next hour and a half we spit shined the place, receiving a pat on the back for a job well done. The drill field was empty and pitch black as we ran back across it toward the barracks laughing about the earlier incident. It was 2230 before we got to bed.

At 0500 on Wednesday morning the routine we were to live by for the next month started. We performed the same ritual of clean up and breaking starch before inspection, followed by an hour of free time; the last half of which was spent either in the latrine or waiting in line for an open stall. By 1000 hours we were warming up at pool side getting ready for the two hundred flutter kicks that we did

69

every day along with the towel and underwater swims. I always made it back to the barracks with over a half mask full of water, but someone was always owing Wilson a hundred push-ups.

By the time we did our pull-ups, went inside to change clothes and fall out on the pull-up bar it was 1115. When we arrived at the chow hall some thirty GIs were standing in line so Carpenter walked right up to the front of the line and grabbed a tray. The airman he cut in front of started to protest, but Carpenter just told him to "Sit down and shut up!"

The airman patiently waited as each of us got our food before him, obviously thinking what ass holes we were. There was no way he could know the tight schedule we had to meet, and we didn't take time to explain it to him. For the next ten minutes we threw food into our mouths and washed it down with milk, swallowing the last bite as we tossed the tray of dirty dishes on the receiving line.

It was 1140 when we regrouped outside in the hot sunshine and ran to the classroom, singing our non-stop repertoire of rescue songs. The drill field was packed with GIs marching to and fro as Carpenter zigzagged us around their columns and occasionally circling one, singing some harassing song about their legs. We entered the building complex that held ours, as well as a hundred other classrooms, and landed in our seats with enough time to wipe the sweat from our faces before 1200 hours.

For the next six hours, with only two short breaks, we studied from the text book entitled, *Emergency Care and Transportation of the Sick and Injured* along with its associated workbook, listened and took notes to some interesting lectures, watched some gory films including childbirth and burns, and had some selected reading from the *Merck Manual.* When we left at 1800 hours the building had been empty for two hours. We were always last to leave, running and singing across the empty drill field on our way back to the chow hall. It was a lonely feeling, and we still had the evening PT to look forward to.

Every weekday was a carbon copy. "Make it through Sheppard, and you'll make it through Pararescue." The words of experience kept coming back to me. The pace of the routine was furious with only nine hours on Sunday afternoon to look forward to rest.

On the third Saturday we were there, my family came to visit. It's a three and a half hour drive from Oklahoma City to Wichita Falls, so they had to leave around 0400 that morning to arrive at the barracks while we were doing push-ups during inspection. They leaned against the car and watched as we recovered and dropped several more times before inspection was over.

"Who are those people?" Wilson asked when he came out to join us.

"Those are my people," I replied.

"Well don't leave mother waiting," he said sympathetically, "go see her."

I ran to them across the lawn, but instead of greeting me with a hug my mother handed me a towel that she had taken from her suitcase. We were sweating so hard they could see it pour off of us from fifty yards away.

"Oh, you look so cute with that blue scarf around your neck," she said as she gave me a big hug. "This uniform is kind of starchy, isn't it?" she half asked and half stated.

"Yeah," I said, "it's kind of starchy."

She wanted to know if my sergeant would let me go with them off base to eat and talk and find something to do. I shook my head and took her by the arm inviting everybody inside to meet sergeant Wilson. He was genuinely pleased to have visitors and warmly welcomed my mother, dad, brother, sister-in-law and their two children.

"You can go get ready for PT now," he told me. "I'll keep your folks company." It was 0930 and the letters "PT" made my bowels move.

They had a choice of staying at the barracks or going to the pool. The films didn't appeal to them as much as watching us do PT. The fact is, they didn't know what to expect because I hadn't told them. I didn't think anyone would believe me, not even my parents. Wilson was all smiles saying, "You can ride over with me. The team will meet us there in a few minutes."

They watched us climb the pull-up bar, but drove off before we finished the set. Grabbing our PT gear, we ran to the pool. In the three weeks that we had been there, we had improved steadily and even the sores on our feet began to callus over. We still used the mole skin and wore socks to prevent the painful blisters from returning. They were waiting for us at the pool side when we entered and took our positions after stowing our gear behind us.

They watched mostly in silence as we hurried our way through the warm-up and in complete silence as we counted

WE'RE ALL MAD, YOU KNOW

out push-ups and sit-ups. Wilson had us lined up close enough for the flutter kicks so that we were only one stride away from each other. When we started, my mothers face was bright and cheery as they pointed at the columns of water we were throwing in unison.

At number twenty-five, Wilson stood on Carpenter's stomach and lightly bounced up and down. He stepped to the next man's stomach, bouncing his one-hundred-ninety-pound body up and down before moving to the next man. When he jumped on me, I was surprised at how easily I held up his weight as he balanced himself and stepped to the next man. He reached the end, heavily turned about face, and ran across our abdomens back to Carpenter before jumping off. The smile on my mother's face turned to dismay and the count was only approaching seventy-five.

Mom must have thought we were going to yell "one for pararescue" at one-hundred-one, because at a hundred and two her mouth dropped open and her eyes widened. Her gaze then turned to Wilson with an anger I had never seen from her before. She stormed over to Wilson with the bravery only a mother can muster and began beating him on the chest, screaming, "Make them stop! Make them stop!"

Dad followed slowly behind her at first, but hustled it up once she started slugging Wilson. He grabbed her by the shoulders, holding her at bay.

Wilson wasn't angry. In fact, he was laughing inside. "Lady, these guys can do this all day long."

My mother and father turned around and watched us count out "one-hundred-and-twenty-five..."

73

WE'RE ALL MAD, YOU KNOW

She was gripping Dad's arm with a somber expression that was getting sadder as the count went on. At one-hundred-fifty our pain was obvious and the knuckles of her hands were turning white as her fingernails dug into Dad's arm. Her bottom lip was beginning to quiver, and at one-seventy-five she was brushing tears off of her cheek and burying her head in Dad's chest, watching from the corner of her wet eyes.

Wilson was eating it up. When we finished two-hundred-one, Wilson had us hold our fins over the water for fifteen more seconds before allowing us to recover. We recovered a lot faster than my mother did.

We performed several trips with the towels for them before the underwater swim and walked past her on the way to the shallow end. After getting my snorkel she whispered to me, "When is this going to end?"

"Two more weeks," I told her knowing that didn't answer her question. My fastest time ever was recorded for the mile swim that morning with me placing third in twenty six minutes and thirty seconds. I had to tread water a little longer but it was worth it to be able to show off in front of my folks. They even got a healthy laugh when they saw us fall-in outside the pool with a mask full of water on our faces, following along behind us in the truck as we ran to the barracks. We knocked out our pull-ups and fell-in at attention with Wilson stern faced as he paced in front of us. His face relaxed and a smile took over as he told me to enjoy the afternoon with my mother, but be back for PT before 1900 hours. It only made sense that he should give the rest of the team the afternoon off as well. We were punished as a team, and rewarded as a team.

WE'RE ALL MAD, YOU KNOW

Dad said he was impressed, not knowing that the Air Force had such an outfit. He had himself been an Army combat medic during WWII but knew of no one that trained this hard. I assured him that I had heard Marine Recon, Seals, and Rangers trained this hard, but we all agreed that the Air Force was an unlikely branch to find this caliber of military discipline. When I told mom I could quit anytime I wanted to, she begged me to quit today. All I could do was laugh.

"I joined this team to jump, dive, climb, and hopefully save somebody's life," I told her. "I can't quit now."

I changed the subject. "So, how's Frank?" I asked about my brother, who had been wounded in Vietnam.

"Not good, Gary. He's going into the VA tomorrow for some experimental surgery on his arm. I sure hope he will be able to use it again someday," she answered, obviously worried.

"If I know Frank, he'll use it again. What else is new?"

"You're not going to believe this one," she said. "They're going to flood Sardis."

Sardis, Oklahoma, is where Mom and Dad met. I had spent summers there most of my life, and, at the age of thirteen, learned to drive along the dirt roads of the narrows between the mountains. Soon, according to Mom, it would be "Sardis Lake," less than a mile from my Uncle Sye McGuire's house.

They say when you return home after a long absence, that it is always different--and you "can never go back." For Sardis, this was proving to be literal fact. All I would have is memories.

WE'RE ALL MAD, YOU KNOW

The afternoon was over in a hurry and I had my folks take me back by 1800, not wanting to take advantage of Wilson's generous good nature. The rest of the team felt the same and they were back when I got there. PT that night wasn't any easier, but our attitude made it much easier to endure. Sergeant Wilson already had our respect, now he had our hearts.

The remaining two weeks went by with the same pain and endurance that we were accustomed to since I started almost three months ago. I was stronger, with muscles rippling in my abdomen, and arms and legs solid as a rock. I was smarter too, in both emergency medicine and doing what I was told,(that is, how to stay out of trouble).

The volume of information we had to memorize regarding anatomy, signs and symptoms, and treatments seemed mind boggling until we began to understand the language of medicine and how to tell the difference between normal and abnormal. Thinking and practicing in a classroom is required learning, but it doesn't mimic real life. For that, you have to go outside.

The day of our EMT final exam had been a long time coming. We took the written test on one day, and the following day we started eighteen hours of practical exercises. For these, we were picked up at 0530 and bussed to a far corner of the base. We lowered each other from trees, made improvised litters and practiced different styles of carrying. We took turns playing victim and rescuer, diagnosing and treating the usual assortment of injuries and illness.

76

WE'RE ALL MAD, YOU KNOW

We ate C-rations for lunch and were given a demonstration of why you don't want to be shot with an M-16. A vacuum packed gallon can of green beans was first shot with an M-1 (which was used during World War II and the Korean war) and it simply made a small hole through the can allowing the juice to leak out. A new can was then shot with the M-16. The can jumped six inches straight up and green beans exploded out the back through the gaping hole torn in the can. It was explained to us that the super high velocity of the 5.56mm (.223 caliber) bullet creates a vacuum as it passes through soft tissue. After ripping the tissue and passing out of the victim's body, a rush of air enters the vacuum of the hole created by the passing bullet before the tissue has time to occupy the space. This in-rush of air is what made the can jump.

In the afternoon we went through an obstacle course designed not so much for endurance, but rather to make us think. We had to cross barricades without touching the sides, and an array of mine fields and other seemingly impossible tasks. Along the way we encountered victims to treat and carry to safety. The exercise proved how difficult it is to think on your feet. The evening culminated with a mock airplane disaster.

We waited long enough after sundown for complete darkness to be only minutes away before running a half mile to where the broken fuselage of an airplane lay. Bodies were strung out for fifty yards around. Even more were inside the airplane. Our victims were GIs that volunteered for the occasion and played their parts realistically, some moaning and some screaming as we set up a triage station a safe distance from the airplane.

WE'RE ALL MAD, YOU KNOW

The first man I came to was making no noise at all. I placed my ear next to his mouth and felt for a pulse in his neck. He finally told me that he was dead after I spent a minute looking for injuries. I was glad, because the darkness was making it frustratingly difficult to find the simulated injuries they had on which were vivid in daylight.

Looking up for my next victim I spotted an ambulance that had been there since we arrived. I ran over to it and asked the attendants if they had any flashlights. "All you had to do was ask," the man told me and flipped a switch that flooded the area with light.

We were taught to sort injured victims into categories according to the severity of the wounds. Victims like my first one were category four, people who are either dead already or are going to die regardless of any treatment given to them. I left him lying there although one or two 'dead men' were carried to the triage area. Category one people, so called 'walking wounded,' were put to work cleaning and bandaging the wounds of category two victims, injuries that were not life threatening but required some sort of intervention. Carpenter stayed at the triage area organizing the chaos and treating category three victims; the most seriously injured people who still had a chance for survival. I don't know how long we spent getting the forty or so victims ready for evacuation, but it sure went by fast. On the bus back to base, the victims all agreed that we had done an excellent job. As much as we appreciated that, nothing made us feel better than knowing we didn't have to do PT in the morning.

WE'RE ALL MAD, YOU KNOW

The whole team had survived thirty eight solid days of busting ass and giving everything we had. Wilson felt that was worth a celebration. He brought more beer and hamburgers than we could possibly eat and drink, so we went out in search of women. The first girl I asked said she was afraid to be around people like us, but the second one said, "Sure, sounds like fun."

This was our last day, and having gotten close to Wilson it was easy to feel comfortable around him, which let us be ourselves. MacMahon said he could drink a can of beer in three seconds and our skepticism made him prove it. He slowly turned a fresh, cold can upside down and poked a hole in the bottom of it with an ice-pick. Holding a finger over the hole, he eased it back upright and popped the top. He took his finger off of the hole as he drank and beer poured out of the can faster than he could drink it. Beer foamed out of his mouth and nose but in three seconds the can was empty. We laughed until our sides ached as everybody grabbed a beer and poked a hole in the bottom. We got as much beer on us as we did in us.

Wilson told us some war stories, and we told some stories about ourselves. But the evening was coming on and we seemed to be running out of things to do. Wilson suggested we go in his office and watch some rescue films. His office was too small to hold this many people comfortably, but we squeezed in. The lights were turned out and we watched a film about a downed pilot being rescued from the jungles of South-East Asia. The mini-guns on board the helicopter were blazing from three positions, the support aircraft were strafing the area with white phosphorous and napalm, and the PJ was riding the jungle penetrator at the end of the hoist to the jungle floor when we thought we heard a knock on the door.

The knock became a bang after an unsuccessful attempt to open the door against the three bodies being pressed against it. "This is the police," a voice outside cried out. "Open this door!"

The people by the door gave way and a hand reached inside and flipped on the lights. Wilson turned off the projector and demanded an explanation. "It's illegal to have female personnel in male barracks," the sky cop said very officially. "You're all under arrest!" and read us our rights.

"This is my office," Wilson stated in a matter-of-fact tone. "It's not like these women were alone in one of the men's rooms."

But his reasoning fell on deaf ears. The sergeant of the Air Police ordered everyone outside and into the back of the three waiting trucks.

Outside we were met with hundreds of eyes from the crowd of bystanders that had gathered around the flashing red lights of all the police vehicles. This must of been the biggest bust ever at Sheppard AFB. None of us were put behind bars, but we did spend an hour standing around the lobby of the cop shop. Wilson had to call a MAC (Military Airlift Command) general in Washington, who had to call a Security Police general, who then called the arresting sergeant before the charges were dropped and we were driven home. It would have been funny under different circumstances, but it spoiled whatever else may have happened that night. All things considered, Wilson knew how to throw a party.

WE'RE ALL MAD, YOU KNOW

Some noise down the hall woke me up and I squinted my eyes to avoid the sunshine that we rarely woke up to. It was 0900. Carpenter was starting up the stairs as I passed by on the way to the latrine.

"Make sure everyone up there is packed and ready for chow by 1130 hours McGuire. Because if they're not I'm holding you responsible."

Carpenter couldn't help but be an ass. He was strong and he was in charge. I went back down the hall waking everybody up before going to the latrine, not wanting to stir Carpenter's wrath.

It didn't take long to put what few possessions we had into our duffel bags and shower and dress. At the chow hall we took our place in the back of the line since we had a whole hour before the bus picked us up. We were used to some people looking at us and some people ignoring us, but something this day was different. We all noticed that the place seemed kind of quiet. The Air Force doesn't mind if GIs talk when they eat so it's noticeable when they don't. One young WAF serving vegetables refused to look up as the guys ahead of me stated their preference. As I got closer I could see the emotion she was expressing in the way she was throwing the food on the plates.

"Is there something the matter?" I asked her when it came my turn, breaking what felt like some pretty thick ice.

"Well, is it true?" she demanded, looking up for the first time. I looked at her, then looked down the line at the rest of the team. Everyone had an expression on their face that said, "I don't know what the hell she's talking about."

WE'RE ALL MAD, YOU KNOW

We all looked at her and she asked, "Were you showing porno films in your barracks last night?"

"Alll-riiight!" Setchfield said spontaneously as everyone was nodding their heads and laughing. We had a reputation to live up to, so no one made an attempt to deny it. We were still laughing when we got on the bus.

Chapter Four

Key West

Nothing could have looked better to us than Sheppard AFB from the rear window of the bus when we left the main gate for the last time. We had said our good-byes to Sergeant Wilson the night before but no matter how much we thought of him, we were damn glad he couldn't torture us anymore. The long months of pre-conditioning had paid off. There was no stopping us now. We were on our way.

We flew out of Wichita Falls and into Dallas where we changed planes for Miami, Florida. It was 1600 hours when we made our descent through the towering clouds that hugged the coast of south Florida. It was May 19th and we were a few days ahead of schedule so instead of catching a bus for Key West like we were supposed to do,

83

we called three taxis and loaded the team and our gear for a short drive to Rick Prado's house.

Rick was born and raised in Miami and his parents and sisters were delighted to have us, although they had no warning we were coming. They listened with keen interest as we told embarrassing stories on Rick as well as bragging on him for his strength and endurance. We all went to dinner together, each of us paying our own way not wanting to impose anymore than we already had.

It was great to have a night in a big city, and Miami has some exciting and unique places to drink and dance. Our short hair made it obvious we were GIs but the girls danced with us anyway. Rick warned us early on not to start or even participate in any trouble. "People in this town carry guns," he told us. We took the hint.

We got in so late that everyone had to find a spot on the floor to pass out on. In the morning Rick's dad saw us off. The pride he felt for his son showed in his face, making the parting that much easier.

It was a long bus ride to the bottom of the keys, making several stops along the way. I kept looking for the everglades but all I could see was an ocean of grass. A civilian passenger told me not to be disappointed because that's what the everglades meant--grasslands. We would ride along for a while in bright sunshine, and then through a torrential rain followed by sunshine again.

We arrived in Key West with just enough time to move our duffel bags into the bus terminal before the next downfall of rain. Carpenter called the Naval Base to provide transportation for the remaining few miles and we pulled up in front of our new home around 1500 hours. As we stepped out the first thing to catch our eye was a statue in front of the barracks of a man wearing SCUBA gear riding a shark. On a large plaque under it was inscribed, "United States Naval Underwater Swimmers School, Key West, Florida."

We had arrived with no fear of what the Navy might do to us. As we collected our gear, Geza Ludanie, who we hadn't seen since Lackland, came bursting out the front door all smiles yelling, "I was looking for you guys yesterday. What happened, you miss a plane?"

We all yelled "Geza!" in complete surprise, not knowing he was going to join our class. His broken arm was healed and the strength in his hand shake proved it.

"What are you doing here, McGuire?" he asked, "I heard your legs were bothering you."

"I don't hurt that bad," I said modestly. The last days at Sheppard were agonizing on my shin splints that wouldn't seem to go away. Wilson offered to let me stay behind to let them rest and join the next class but the thought of another forty-five days of PT made me realize that I could run with a little pain.

Geza showed us to our bunks in the upstairs open bay barracks. Mosquito netting covered the open windows surrounding a large room with thirty bunk beds, most of them already taken. The majority of the students were Navy, hoping to join a SEAL Team. Three Marines were training for Recon. One other student in this class didn't live in the barracks with us but he too was Air Force. He was a captain and soon would be one of only five officers in the entire Air Force to wear a maroon beret. He was training to be a Pararescue Officer.

85

WE'RE ALL MAD, YOU KNOW

The captain didn't exactly look like a Charles Atlas, but then neither did we. We were to find out he was a hard man to keep up with.

Lieutenant Bates, on the other hand, did resemble Charles and he was the Navy Officer in charge of PT. Monday morning Lt. Bates lead a toned-down version of the exercises we were accustomed to. We were completing each set so far ahead of the Navy that we spent a lot of time waiting for everyone to catch up. The Marines weren't breaking much of a sweat either. Most of these Navy guys were fresh out of basic, and I remembered a few months back how I looked doing PT.

The workout was tough enough to make, and half of them quit before the end of the first week. During a run one morning, Geza started giving the Navy boys a hard time even though the pace was seven-and-a-half minutes per mile, prompting Lt. Bates to order, "OK Air Force, fall out and drop for ten then catch back up."

"Thanks Geza," was all we said as we knocked them out and sprinted to rejoin the formation. Lt. Bates enjoyed it so much we found ourselves dropping several times during each run for much of the first week.

One pool workout consisted of an exercise where we carried an empty bucket on our chest while swimming on our backs without fins. The bucket had an open wide mouth that instantly filled with water and created enough drag to make the forward progress so slow that everyone was out of breath after twenty-five yards.

We were paired up and the two partners had to stay together or be tied to each other by the buddy rope. A heavy braided line five feet long with loops at each end hung around the necks of those that couldn't stay together. Of the several instructors we have had, Sergeant Sweeney was the most colorful. He was said to have been decorated on numerous occasions in Southeast Asia for acts of bravery and heroism but was busted as fast as he could gain rank due to misbehaving. They said he rode a horse into a bar somewhere and grabbed a barmaid, then rode off with her after doing considerable damage to the bar. He looked the part.

Classroom instruction was five hours a day, studying from the impressive US Navy diving manual. I did pay attention in class as Boyle's, Charles', Dalton's and Henry's laws were discussed in detail as pertaining to SCUBA diving. Having taught some small classes myself, the information was just a refresher until they got to the more advanced studies of operating a recompression chamber and computing repetitive dives so we wouldn't need one.

My intent here is not to instruct SCUBA but basically to point out some of the more interesting phenomenon. A common misconception is that coming up too fast causes the bends. The truth is, only after staying deeper than thirty-three feet for longer than the no decompression limit for the deepest point of that dive, and returning to the surface without making the necessary decompression stop(s) will result in the rapid release of nitrogen bubbles from the supersaturated blood stream and body tissue. To avoid the bends, or Cason's disease as it's sometimes called, you either never go below thirty-three feet, or plan your dive carefully knowing the deepest depth you intend to make and compute the entire dive as if it were from that depth. That gives you a little extra room for error.

Spontaneous pneumothorax is the term given to explain what really happens when a diver ascends too fast. Usually he has panicked and holds his breath as he races for the surface. The decreasing water depth also decreases the absolute pressure causing the ten pints of compressed air breathed from the tank into his lungs to expand proportionately. You need only rise eight feet before the expanding air ruptures the alveoli of the lungs.

Nitrogen does more to the SCUBA diver than just cause the bends. Beginning between the depths of ninety and one hundred ten feet, the partial pressure of nitrogen becomes so great that it produces a narcotic effect on the brain that grows in intensity the deeper you go. Signs and symptoms range from ringing in the ears to dizziness and euphoria that borders on foolishness. Some people are so sensitive to the effects that they become nauseated and vomit through their regulator. At one hundred thirty feet, that can be lethal.

Oxygen itself can kill a SCUBA diver. There is enough of it in the air we breathe for its partial pressure at two hundred ninety seven feet to be lethal. It's necessary to reduce the amount of oxygen as well as replace the nitrogen with the more inert gas, helium, to eliminate the narcosis on dives approaching or exceeding two hundred ninety-seven feet. Therapeutic oxygen becomes lethal at only twenty-five feet limiting oxygen re-breathing units to a maximum depth of fifteen feet. But re-breathers do not produce any bubbles and are great for sneaking up on somebody.

WE'RE ALL MAD, YOU KNOW

As inherently dangerous as SCUBA diving is, salt water adds a dimension of death not found in fresh water. In fresh water, man is the meanest creature to be found, with the possible exceptions of pirahana, alligators and crocadiles. In salt water, man is just another meal to creatures such as Great White sharks. Many other creatures are potentially more lethal due to their numbers and camouflage. The rock, or scorpion fish lies invisible on the bottom with its spines filled with deadly poison sticking straight up, easily stepped on or grabbed by accident. An antidote does exist but you're dead before you can get out of the water. The list includes sea snakes, lion fish, and even small cone shells housing critters with lethal stings. The sight of a barracuda will humble the meanest of men.

The building we held class in had a freshwater tank that was eight feet by eight feet and twenty feet deep. One at a time, we swam to the bottom, equalizing our ear pressure every few feet by using the val-salva maneuver. This is done by simply holding and blowing into your nose, forcing air through the Eustachian tube to the middle ear. We swam under a glass partition into a compartment tall enough to stand in and half filled with compressed air. An instructor was there to remind us that we were breathing compressed air and to ascend slowly, exhaling to avoid the dreaded pneumothorax.

That turned out to be a practice run. The next day we went to a pier that had a rope tied to the dock which extended into the water. A compressor was pumping air through lines that followed the same path as the rope. One at a time we entered the water wearing mask and swim suite, disappearing beneath the surface as we followed the rope down.

Geza was just ahead of me in line. When he surfaced and peeled off his mask, blood poured out of it.

"Oh my God, I'm dying!" he cried out. A few minutes of direct pressure stopped the bleeding that was coming from his nose. I would be guessing at what may have caused it but he really was all right and I was told to go ahead on down the line.

I followed the line down, which stretched out at an angle that ran thirty feet out from the pier to a thirty foot deep chamber that one of the lines was feeding air to. An instructor inside the chamber made sure I had caught my breath before sending me on down the line that ran back toward the pier and to a depth of fifty feet. I swam under the bell to be greeted by Sweeney who bluntly asked, "You OK?"

"Fine," I answered.

"Then quit breathing my air."

I took one more lung full as I lifted my body a little higher out of the water and streamlined it to dip under the lip of the bell. I looked up as I let go of the bell, lightly flutter kicking my legs as I pursed my lips to exhale a small stream of bubbles as I started for the surface. The water was murky and at first I was unable to see the surface. But the shimmering light grew steadily brighter as my body drifted upward.

The rule of thumb for how fast to surface is no faster than the smallest bubbles which is close to the text book answer of one foot per second. The water grew lighter and the stream of bubbles continued to flow as the surface became distinguishable. During the last fifteen feet of ascent I had to control the urge to hurry to the top and breathe. Our training at Sheppard taught us something about control, and now that training came in handy. We spent a lot of time in the pool doing PT and swimming. We didn't dive for the first week, and didn't start clearing our mask and snorkels until Friday. But Monday we were introduced to our SCUBA tanks. The twin seventy-two cubic foot bottles provided us with over two hours of diving time, which we used to scrub every square inch of the bottom of the pool.

Tuesday and Wednesday were spent practicing "ditch and don" techniques and buddy breathing. "Ditch and don" is the ability to take off and put back on all of our equipment underwater. It's easy enough when you can see what you're doing, but we had to be good enough to do it in the dark.

Thursday came the infamous "panic test." Our masks were lined with aluminum foil, and for the next thirty minutes the instructors harassed us by turning off our air, pulling off our masks, unbuckling the harness, and jerking the tanks off our backs attempting to make us panic. We agreed that one of the instructors was malicious, but we couldn't see who was doing what.

Friday afternoon we made our first open water dive, having to lug the tanks on our backs two hundred yards to the end of a pier. We entered the water in teams of five, making a ten foot free-fall from the pier. The Navy man standing beside me didn't hold his mask to his face as he entered the water. I looked down in time to see it sink out of sight. Four of us started down at the same time to

91

retrieve it, but when I reached the bottom at fifty-five feet, I was alone. I looked up to see two men hovering at the fringe of visibility but they weren't coming the rest of the way down. I didn't blame them because it was eerie, dark and cold down there. Huge wooden posts leered only a few feet away holding a blackness even darker than the water around me. I imagined the monsters of folklore, and shuddered a little thinking how easy it would be to believe such stories. The mask took a minute to find against the bottom and I was happy when I spotted it. I grabbed the mask and headed for the surface before "the monster" realized I was there.

"Don't worry about it," I told him as I handed it over.

We spent a leisurely hour swimming under the ships that were docked in the yard, darting through the huge screws that propelled them. Knowing that "divers are down" stopped all movement going in or out of the cove that protected the dock, but I was still uneasy about being this close to them. Some were as big as airplane propellers, and the possibility of someone not getting the word and starting an engine kept me from lingering too long. Still, I was fascinated by the massive machinery. I remembered my amazement at learning the principle behind the movement of not only ships but airplanes as well. Whether your talking ships screws, airplane propellers or a helicopters rotor, your talking about a wing. Air or water flows faster across the top or front side than it does the bottom or back side, creating a slightly lower pressure on the top or front. That causes the wing (screw, propeller, blade) to attempt to occupy the area of less pressure producing lift or momentum.

WE'RE ALL MAD, YOU KNOW

Our dive ended at the beginning of the pier where we surfaced at a boat ramp. We took off our fins and walked up the ramp out of the water, lugging the tanks a quarter of a mile to the wash racks. It was Friday afternoon and I needed every minute of rest that my lower legs could get.

Phil Parker nearly didn't make the team. He was certainly large, strong, and fast enough, it was just that he was missing the tip of his left ring finger. It took a high level decision, with approval from the flight surgeon to allow him to stay in. He was a better than average pool shooter and to beat him was something to brag about. A table was downstairs in the basement, and this Saturday morning, Phil was taking in a little money, including three hundred dollars from one of the instructors.

We were taken to open water Monday afternoon for a twenty minute dive at ninety feet with a brief decompression stop at ten feet. The water out from the Key's increased in depth so gradually that we had to travel over two miles out to find water that deep. We went over the side of the landing craft in groups of eight, including the instructor. The power of the Gulf stream took us away from the landing craft, and the line we were to follow to the bottom. We were forced to swim back up-stream to regroup at the line before descending as a team. The current was equally as strong on the bottom and was a constant force to contend with.

Our instructor stretched a line out from the anchor as each man waited for a knot to grab and swim out with the line. Although visibility was good, it was not great. From the middle I could not see the two ends, only the two people on either side of me. We swam in a circle around the anchor and it wasn't long before I saw a scorpion fish camouflaged among the rocks. I had seen them before in the Gulf of California off of Guymas, Mexico, so I knew how to spot them. But I knew the inexperienced divers wouldn't know one even if they could see it, so I jerked on the line to signal the others to come see. It took a minute for everyone to arrive and even longer to see the deadly fish laying on the bottom. I prodded it with my knife and it moved a few feet before settling down again.

The instructor stretched the line back out and everyone resumed their previous positions before continuing to swim around the anchor. The bottom was flat and sandy, with little more than a few rocks scattered around, so there wasn't much to see. A sting ray lazily skimmed near the bottom, apparently aroused by our presence and was soon beyond my visibility. We were too shallow to feel the effects of nitrogen narcosis and too deep for most sea life. If it weren't for the thrill of being in an alien environment and feeling the sensations of weightlessness, it would have been boring. The next group hit the water as soon as we surfaced.

We had taken our written test the morning before the pier dive. Instead of attending class after PT, we loaded in the landing craft for the next three days for compass swims. The first swim was five hundred yards, the second was seven hundred fifty yards and the third was one thousand yards. We entered the water in two man teams, one man holding a compass attached to a stick. The other man had a buoy line attached to him so the instructors could monitor our progress. We were given one minute to sight the target on shore and determine the heading. From there it was necessary to swim straight down to the bottom, find the heading and swim a straight line to the target. Again I had the advantage since my old SCUBA club practiced the same thing, only with shorter distances. I missed dead reckoning by ten yards on my best attempt and was within twenty yards even on the final swim of fifteen hundred yards. Even though some people had no experience at all with following a compass, I still couldn't understand how they missed the mark by nearly two hundred yards.

Our third swim was from one thousand yards, made at night. Our target was a light on the beach, which made it easy to find the heading before dropping forty five feet to the bottom. The florescent dial of the compass made keeping the course as easy as during the day. In all fairness, holding the handle on the compass steady out in front of you while swimming is not possible. The degree indicator bounces slightly up and down in the friction free fluid and is extremely sensitive to minute changes in direction. The secret is to produce a steady flutter kick, taking a moment before starting to completely neutralize your buoyancy. If you begin to float upward, simply put a rock in your shorts. If you start to sink, put a little air in your life vest through the manual inflation value. The heading will still drift to one side, so you have to overcorrect an equal amount for the same length of time before bringing it back on course.

We hated to see this school end even though it did mean another party. The Marines, as gung ho and fearless as their reputation, with a little help, dunked Lieutenant Bates in the ice cold water that remained in the tub after all the beer was drank. This had been sheer bliss and I began to miss the ocean and beach and weather before we even left. But on June 18th, leave we did.

For jump school.

Splashdown for McGuire in the South China Sea. Okinawa's "Suicide Cliffs" show in the background. Shroud lines from right side of risers have been jettisoned to prevent chute from dragging the jumper. (Photo by Bill Robbins)

Sgt. Gary McGuire, wearing SCUBA gear, jumps from a C-130 over the South China Sea. His parachute canopy is beginning to deploy behind the airplane. (Photo by Bill Robbins)

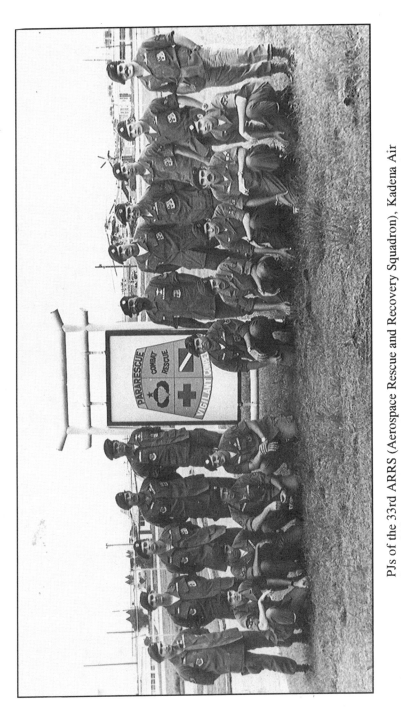

PJs of the 33rd ARRS (Aerospace Rescue and Recovery Squadron), Kadena Air Base, Okinawa, 1975. HH-3E spotted for scramble rests on the ramp behind Gary McGuire, third from right, top row. (Photo by Bill Robbins)

HH-3E rescue helicopter 777 just before retirement. PJ Sergeant Gary McGuire is securing sling load for practice pick-up. PJs had to be versed in all types of sling load and winch operation. (Photo by Bill Robbins)

A1C Ed Setchfield, January 1973. Gear includes main parachute and SCUBA tanks (twin 42 cu. ft.), mask, regulater, reserve parachute, medical kit, one-man life raft with survival gear, dive knife, snorkel, Mark 13 flare, depth gauge, watch, and compass. Total weight of gear: 150 lbs. (USAF photo)

PJ Class 72-04, Sheppard AFB. L to R, top row: Setchfield, Dunlap, Aldridge, McLafferty, Mac Mahon, Aldean (visiting), Birkland, Carpenter, Parker, McGuire. Bottom row: Prado, four medical instructors, Hutchinson. We were ordered to smile. (USAF photo)

Chapter Five

Fort Benning

Columbus, Georgia was only a few hours North by air but nothing could turn the calendar back. We noticed, while reading our orders out front of the locked building we were to report to, that we should have been here the day before yesterday. We stayed for the party not realizing that jump school enrollment ended the same day SCUBA school ended.

We found a pay phone, and Carpenter called Colvert at home in San Antonio. He explained our predicament and repeated the number to the phone booth several times before hanging up. It was a half hour later before it rang. Carpenter was given a building number, and he made one more call for taxis to take us there. Two soldiers arrived and they got us processed in and assigned to barracks, then told us we missed the deadline and would start with a new class in one week.

"Where's your phone?" Carpenter demanded, and had Colvert on the phone within a minute. Word came back that we were to start with the next morning's class.

It wasn't a far walk from there to our barracks. From the moment we came on the Fort we felt like we had entered the Twilight Zone. Two large towers with four umbrellas poking out at the top, loomed in the distance. All the buildings looked as if they came out of Beetle Bailey and many, including our barracks, were pre-WWII vintage. Both floors were open bays with lockers and bunk beds. This was the most depressing place I had ever stayed in.

We had enough time to unpack and find the chow hall. The Army had plenty of food, it just wasn't what we were used to. Navy chow was the best and the Air Force a close second. I never had Marine chow, and not much of the Army's. We found a hamburger stand not far away.

We were supposed to get up at 0500 hours to square our areas away and be ready to fall out in formation at 0600 hours. That only took us fifteen minutes so I slept till 0530 a lot. Three Airborne classes were being instructed at the same time and some four hundred people fell out for roll call. Because we arrived late we Air Force guys were the only ones without steel helmets. This made us stand out even more than our differences in uniform. The helmets soon came and a number was taped across the front. Several instructors walked among us with an aide carrying a clipboard. They looked for buttons unbuttoned and lose threads, having the aide denote the discrepancy with a demerit. We laughed all morning about the demerits we had received.

The inspection was over in thirty minutes, giving us over an hour to get through the chow hall line for some crummy eggs and biscuits. Geza's voice carried and his accent was picked up by an Army guy several men ahead of us in line. The GI was Geza's size and walked up to him saying, "The last guy that made fun of the way I talk picked up his teeth with a broken arm."

Things were quiet for a moment as they looked at each other, but Geza knew a Hungarian when he saw one and said something in Hungarian. The other man smiled big and spoke back something only Geza could understand. They were good friends for the three short weeks of Jump School.

At 0800 we were back in formation for a three mile run at a pace called the Airborne Shuffle. The pace was slow, maybe eight minutes per mile while singing GI marching songs. Running along the back roads of the fort, my shin splints kept me in agony.

PT consisted of eight pull-ups, some push-ups and sit-ups, but everyone including the five women in the class had no difficulty. Our biggest concern was getting out of shape because sooner or later, PJ instructors would get their hands on us again.

From there we were split up into the three classes that went separate directions. Over one hundred of us went to the saw dust pit. The sweat came easy in the hot June mornings. I was glad the amount of PT was so much less than Sheppard because the saw dust stuck to us bad enough as it was. The itchy stuff found it's way under our collar and under the blousing bands on our calves. It even got under the waist band of our shorts.

The purpose for being in the saw dust was necessary enough, but we were there all day, everyday for the entire week practicing parachute landing falls, or PLF's as they were referred to. The object is to let the meaty parts of your body absorb the landing by rolling. You can do a PLF forward, backward, left or right by twisting your trunk into the direction of drift the instant the balls of your feet hit the ground. As the side of your calf hits the ground, you throw your hip into it while tilting your head and shoulders away from the fall. This makes your body act like a rocking chair as your body rolls past your thighs and hips, and completes the roll by throwing your legs on over with the forward momentum. Your arms have been raised over your head the whole time where they held on to the parachute risers. We would all lay where we had fallen until the instructors told us to recover. We would jump to attention, slap our palms to our thighs, and yell "Clear sergeant, Airborne." Anytime we were talked to by an instructor, the response was always, "That's clear, sergeant."

Punishment for making a mistake or doing something stupid was to be ordered to "beat your boots." We were beating our boots several times per hour, bending at the knee and slapping the sides of the boot then standing back up, repeating this ten times. The Army people were treating all this very seriously, but we PJ trainees found it to be embarrassing.

In an effort to break up the monotony, they had us jumping off of two-foot and four-foot tall platforms in all directions to perform our PLFs. There was no need to practice from greater than that. Needless to say, by weeks end, everyone could do a PLF.

Over the weekend I read a book about a Green Beret lieutenant in Vietnam named Nick Rowe that was captured by the Vietcong. He described the fire-fight before his capture and the four years he endured as a POW before his escape. I was soon to get a taste of what that might be like. We spent most of the second week in line waiting for our turn to ride one of the many machines. There was the swing line trainer for emergency procedures and the "crash and burn" machine that ended up breaking Geza's arm. It began on a six foot platform where we buckled into a jump harness attached to a trolley on an inclined plane. We rode it in all four directions, not knowing when the instructor would electronically release the harness from the trolley. The machine simulated a ten mph wind to the impact.

On Wednesday morning we were assembled in a stadium for two demonstrations. First, the Army's free-fall parachute team, The Golden Knight's, jumped from five thousand feet so we could see them exit the plane and fall for about twenty seconds before pulling their rip-chords and floating down under Para-commando canopies to a stand-up landing on the pitcher's mound. Second, two dummies were lifted to the top of the drop tower. The first one was dropped free-fall taking three and a half seconds to hit the ground and bounced slightly. The second one was dropped with a parachute in the cigarette roll malfunction taking only a second longer to crash into the ground. That gave us something to think about.

WE'RE ALL MAD, YOU KNOW

From there we practiced jumping out of a C-130 airplane door, one foot off the ground before moving up to the thirty-foot tower. We wore parachute harnesses that we snapped the risers into, which was attached to a trolley on a long cable to the ground at the top of a mound fifty yards away. We only fell four to six feet but it was more than one Army man could take as he broke down crying in the door refusing to jump. It's better that it happened there than at three thousand feet.

Thursday we were attached to old Parachutes and old metal skids that we laid down on, on our backs. A large wind fan was turned on inflating the parachute and dragging us for a rough ride about twenty feet before we could pull the capewell. This exposed the steel wire 'D' ring that, when pulled, released the parachute from the harness, thus deflating the canopy. You can't hold an inflated parachute against a wind stronger than ten mph.

Friday we met at the bottom of the drop tower. It took all day for each of us to ride it once, but was so much fun we all wanted to do it again. A modified parachute hooked loosely to rings around the edge of the concave lifting mechanism. Once the parachute was in place, the operator lifted it high enough to let the suspension lines and risers come free from the ground. The jumper stepped under it and an instructor made sure he snapped the risers correctly into the harness capewells before signaling the operator to take them on up.

I remember the ride up as being comfortable. Sitting in a parachute harness is like sitting in a rocking chair. I looked down and around as people got smaller and the expanding horizon got larger. From the top we stayed motionless for a minute taking in the view of the fort and down-town Columbus while thinking about what we were supposed to do when we were released. On command we detached the safety lanyard, and the machine pulled us up another ten feet, where a device was triggered to release all the rings at the same time.

The sensation of the bottom falling out from under me was very pronounced. It lasted only a moment before the drag of the parachute slowed me down. I pulled down hard on the right risers which dumps air out of the opposite side which makes the canopy turn, moving me away from the tower. It took about twenty seconds to descend into the plowed field. I did a PLF, then hustled the 'chute back to be reloaded for the next man. The Army had done everything possible to prepare us, so come next week, we would be jumping for real.

Phil Parker lived in Charleston, South Carolina and over the weekend Tom McLafferty, Ed Setchfield and myself went with him on a bus to see his folks. Any meal would beat Army chow, but home cooking was a rare treat which we enjoyed immensely, trying to remember our manners. Friday night we hopped from bar to bar being refused by some because we were all under twenty one. We had a good time in the ones we got in, but after six months of almost no women, it was hard to make conversation with them. Saturday we took Phil's folks' boat out to the river and water skied up and down it all day. We found some new bars to check out that night, but Sunday morning came and we had a plane to jump out of. Phil's Dad owned a used car lot, and he sold us an old junker for one hundred dollars that got us back to Fort Benning before nightfall.

Monday morning everyone was ready to jump, and were disappointed to find out that we would practice emergency procedures and exit drills all day with the first jump not coming until Tuesday. There are a few things that could go wrong while in the aircraft. One is accidental deployment of the reserve parachute. The left arm rests over the reserve pack, holding on to the rip-chord handle to prevent accidental deployment. In the event it should deploy and get away, you're supposed to follow whatever path the pilot 'chute takes out the aircraft, and do it fast even if it goes under seats and over cables. Once everything deploys it's going to pull you through whatever obstacle you haven't cleared yet.

Rarely, the parachute will hang up on something on the outside of the aircraft's skin or possibly the 80# test chord tying the apex to the static line won't break, meaning the rigger used 800# test chord by mistake. It has been known to happen. The hung jumper is supposed to place one hand over the reserve handle and the other hand on top of his helmet to indicate he is conscious and ready to be cut free. If he can't be cut free the runway will be foamed by the fire department and the aircraft will land, dragging the hung jumper from behind.

Even if everything goes right and you manage to exit the aircraft you will be slammed against the side of the jump door if you don't jump hard enough up and out into the one hundred-forty mph wind of the speed of the airplane. The harder you hit the door, the faster you spin and in the frictionless atmosphere the only thing to slow down the spin is the spring like coil of the wound up suspension lines. The result is a streamer or cigarette roll. If it's wound less than one half the way up, you yank apart on the risers and bicycle your legs to untwist yourself. But more than half the way up to the skirt of the canopy, depending on your altitude, you either release both capwells and both 'D' rings to jettison the canopy before deploying the reserve, or hold the pack closed while pulling the reserve rip-chord. You then throw the rip-chord away and reach into the reserve pack and grab a handful of parachute, throwing it out into the direction of the spin. Clearing the door is only half of it. The rigger packs a lot of 'chutes every day, and carelessly stowing the shroud lines can cause the same malfunction.

Then there's the "Mae-West," or "Dolly Parton" as it is sometimes referred to. These occur because one or more shroud lines loops over the top of the canopy, creating two large sections of canopy resembling the actress's cleavage. This creates reduced drag, making you fall faster than is safe. The treatment is "action," jettisoning the main 'chute and deploying the reserve.

That day ended with one more practice run through of hook-up and exit drills. The next morning we were issued parachutes with twenty-four foot static lines. Everyone checked and rechecked the packing dates and hardware, then checking and rechecking the straps and cotter keys.

We sat down on the concrete slab that extended out to the taxiways and runways waiting for the jump aircraft to arrive. Reserve units from around the nation flew in for the training of dropping jumpers.

WE'RE ALL MAD, YOU KNOW

All of our practicing was geared to jumping from C-130 turboprop transport planes, and in flew two C-141s, which were four-engine jet transports. It was planned that way since the 141 is easier to exit because the jump door is located behind the curve of the tail section, protecting it from the wind. By being located more toward the rear, a small hop is all it takes and the airplane will fly out from under you. This would also be the only jump with a twenty four foot static line, going to a twelve-foot static line for all the other jumps. The extra length for the first jump was to let us feel some degree of acceleration.

It was hot that afternoon, but nothing compared to the blast of jet exhaust that we walked through behind the aircraft to enter the cargo bay up the ramp. We were packed in the airplane with no spare room left. Seats lined each wall, and a row of back-to-back seats ran the length of the aircraft down the middle. The only time we took our hands off the reserve handle was to buckle the seat belt and bind the cotter pin of the static line.

We were airborne within only a few minutes and apprehension was apparent. Both jump doors were opened. From one thousand feet the spotter chutes were dropped to determine the wind drift for the jump run. We then climbed to three thousand feet. During the ascent the jumpmaster raised both hands ordering, "Stand up."

He hooked a finger and flexed his arm signaling the order to "hook up." The steel static line cable ran head high, down both sides of the airplane. Everyone jerked and pulled on the hook and re-bent the cotter pin that prevented the hook from coming loose. "Check equipment" we were

WE'RE ALL MAD, YOU KNOW

ordered one last time. We couldn't be more ready, so why was I so scared?

The jumpmaster got down on his hands and knees to look out the door. Every five seconds he signaled for minor course corrections. He then signaled "steady" and slapped the jump platform twice. This ordered the first man to step into the door, and the rest of us shuffled a little closer. For an intense moment we stood poised waiting for the count. The first man showed true grit in his steadiness and movement without hesitation when the jumpmaster slapped him sharply on his hip. We stepped to the platform, got set and stepped into the open air. I thought briefly about the rigger that packed my 'chute as I looked down three thousand feet to the ground below. It was too late to change my mind because I had already entered the void.

We were supposed to count to four, but I couldn't even remember my name. I do remember feeling the hot wind of the jet blast after falling below the belly of the plane and being tossed and jerked, but just as I was picking up speed I felt the tug of the risers pull on the harness and I looked up in time to see the parachute billow out into a beautiful wide open canopy. The next sensation to strike me was the quiet that contrasted sharply from the screaming jet engines of just a few seconds ago.

The sky was stair-stepped with parachutes four rows wide, and still people were jumping from the two C-141s flying in formation. The sky over Fort Benning was littered with parachutes, and out of this many, some malfunctions are expected. Two jumpers came down under reserves after their mains developed Mae-Wests.

The ride to the ground made everything I had gone through to get here worthwhile. We floated toward the ground for five minutes, making a turn into the wind at two hundred feet and prepared to make contact with the ground. You're supposed to look out at the horizon, knees slightly bent and enough tension to overcome the surprise when the balls of your feet touch. Watching the ground will make your legs draw up uncontrollably resulting in a feet, knees, and head landing.

As we hit the ground we recovered immediately and ran to the parachute, avoiding the other jumpers. We daisy-chained the suspension lines and 'S' folded the parachutes in our arms before running across the field to waiting trucks to stow our gear. We were all looking forward to doing it again.

It took three C-130s to hold all of us the following day, and we would now use the twelve foot static line. Many of the same feelings of apprehension were there, but having the first jump behind us it wasn't as severe. The C-130 turbo prop had a more rugged appearance than the C-141s, and the engines sounded different. I somehow felt more at home in the 130. The wind gushing into the door was not a big obstacle to overcome, but you did have to put some leg into jumping against it.

Once outside, instead of counting to four, I looked up to watch the parachute unfolding out of the pack. I was behind the aircraft when the static line broke free of the apex but the parachute, being so light, whipped backward in the prop wash and sailed past me pulling on the harness when it extended parallel to me. Only then did the skirt begin to separate, allowing the canopy to start catching air.

WE'RE ALL MAD, YOU KNOW

The suspension lines started spreading apart and I felt myself swinging down under the inflating parachute. From catching a little air slowly, it was now catching a lot of air fast and popped open just like it was supposed to.

Thursday we made our third jump, adding combat gear to increase our weight, which made the exit a little more difficult. The landing was a little bit rougher, but our only complaint was that time was now moving too fast.

Friday morning we made our fourth jump, hustled to the chow hall, then back to gear up for the fifth and final jump that afternoon. After the last PLF and stowing our gear, we fell in at attention for the graduation ceremony. Some officer gave us a speech about bravery, God and country before congratulating us, then gave the order to pin on the wings.

Several officers fanned out, pinning the silver jump wings on our fatigues, saluting and moving on. That ended the ceremony, and also ended airborne jump school. Our diplomas were mailed to Hill AFB in Utah, and we got the hell out of Fort Benning, Georgia.

Chapter Six

Survival School

It was July 6, 1972 when we left the Army behind, and fifty days since we ate Air Force chow. Fairchild was supposed to be a "piece of cake" school, giving us two weeks to rest up before we had to face PJ instructors again. It turned into a long two weeks crammed with information and experiences useful to staying alive.

We traveled the whole night, catching taxis to take us from Fort Benning to the Columbus Airport, where we flew out to Atlantic City before crossing the length of the US to Spokane, Washington. Carpenter called the base, and an hour later a bus arrived to complete the trip to the 3636 Combat Crew Training Wing. We had the feeling we were being hi-jacked because the driver took some back roads to a secluded, obscure site at the back of the huge grounds that was so remote we never saw the main base.

There were four, two-story brick barracks, an auditorium, and a chow hall. We checked in at an office and were assigned rooms. How they decided that Carpenter and I should share the same room, I don't know but they wouldn't let us change with anyone else so we were stuck. It turned out to be the best thing that could happen to us because we did have some things in common and managed to become good friends.

It was an odd situation having over one hundred students, all of which were officers except the PJs, five flight mechanics, and a few load-masters. With few exceptions, all of our instructors were enlisted men. Three of them were former PJ trainees from the class ahead of us, but were washed out. One was caught wearing contact lenses. It was good to see them again, but was a sad reunion. They wanted to be PJs. With so many officers around we found ourselves saluting continuously.

Classes didn't start until Tuesday, giving my legs the rest they had been needing for three months. We had only two inspections the entire two weeks. There was not one PT session and no running. The first three mornings were spent in the auditorium for classes on such things as how to enter aircraft from the ground, when and how to use pyrotechnic devices, what you can and cannot eat, how to make a wide assortment of improvised tools, shelters and traps, and how to read a map and use a compass. In the afternoons we went outside for hands-on practice of the skills taught in class. We PJ students were assigned to instruct PLF training, and in an hour and a half we had everybody doing them perfectly.

The fourth morning we loaded into three busses and drove to within twenty miles of the Canadian border to the base of a mountain they call Calispell. We were divided into groups of eleven men each, with only one PJ per group. Each group leader was given a map and compass heading. To sustain us for three days, we were each issued a canteen of water, four Long Range Patrol Rations(LRPs), and a panel cut from a parachute with some shroud line attached. We split up going in the same general direction, but after four hours of steady walking, we found our groups to be pretty far away from each other.

The terrain was rugged as we crossed it in single file. A major took the lead first, followed by the rest of us according to our rank, placing me last in line. I was to count the steps and tie a knot in a line when my left foot hit the ground one hundred times. Nearing the tenth knot I called for the Lieutenant in front of me to pass along the message that reached the major and the instructor at the front. The major fell out of line and waited for me to pass and fell in behind me. I nodded to him as I handed him the rope with the knots untied. He nodded back.

It was almost my turn before we found a stream. When my turn did come, we were entering a steep uphill grade that was heavily wooded with thick underbrush and fallen trees. The object was to locate particular check points by holding your compass to north, then looking in the direction of the heading on the map, pick out a prominent landmark as far in the distance as you can see and walk to it. Once there, another compass heading was taken for the next landmark and you're off again. My problem was that I could only see about twenty yards at best, and sometimes only from tree to tree. The going was slow and difficult and we were half way through the major's second turn before we came out of it. Before long we came upon a small camp that was our first check point. We celebrated the occasion by eating an entire LRP.

The days were lasting eighteen hours. We used every daylight hour finding the next checkpoint, setting our lean-to's up in the dark and using pine boughs for a bed. We built a smoke rack and our instructor broke out some beef that he had been packing. We cut it into thin strips, salted it, and hung it up to dry. We then built and baited our traps.

After meeting back at the smoke rack, we were divided into four groups. Each group received a map, flashlight, and compass. We walked in a triangle according to preset headings. Each leg was three hundred yards and each man took the lead for one leg of the walk. We had the advantage of a full moon and found our landmarks with ease. I got back to my leant-to, checked my trap (which was empty), ate a cornflake bar and drank a little of my water.

My stomach felt empty the next morning. I ate the rest of a LRP and made some instant coffee, using all but a swallow of my remaining water. We took only a few minutes to break down the lean-to's and smoke rack. The meat was soft and smelled terrible. I threw mine away.

We had been walking since breakfast before we crossed a creek in the early afternoon. Everyone drank their fill and re-filled our canteens. The thought of parasites crossed

113

my mind, but I was thirsty and couldn't wait for the water purification tablets to take effect. We walked on until nearly dark, gaining several thousand feet in altitude before making camp and setting traps. The instructor came up with a live rabbit and asked if anyone was hungry. Several people volunteered to kill the animal, but the instructor killed it to show us the right way. He held it upside down by the hind feet and karate chopped it in the back of the neck. The animal died immediately without a struggle, it was then skinned, gutted and roasted. The taste was delicious, but a taste was all we got. One rabbit doesn't divide very far between eleven people. Before I went to bed I ate half of another LRP and drank all but a little of my water. My body was conserving water.

The whole next day we walked up and down a series of rolling hills with Mt. Calispell always looming above us in the near distance. Occasionally an "enemy" helicopter would fly over looking for us, but the noise gave us time to take cover and stay still until it passed. We got lost for a few hours, walking past a check point by a hundred yards or better. That put us late getting to the last check point and we had to build our lean-to's in the dark.

I was hungry and had only one more LRP left. We didn't get any surprises that night so I ate part of the last one before I went to sleep, part of it when I woke up, and the last of it before we made camp.

During the walk we passed some berries and stopped to eat a bunch of them. I drank a lot of water from a steam but that didn't help the burning pain of hunger that evening. The instructor offered me a large white onion. I only intended to take one small bite, just to put something

114

in my stomach, but it tasted so sweet I took a second and bigger bite, followed by another, until it was all gone. For five minutes I felt full and satisfied but that turned into a blotted cramp that escalated until I thought I was going to die. All I could do was crawl into my lean to, curl up in the fetal position and moan. I swore I would never eat another onion.

I still hurt the next morning, but we broke camp quickly and walked a few hundred yards to some waiting helicopters. We were sure glad to see them, and rode back to base in silence. The flight took thirty minutes, getting us back in time for breakfast at the chow hall. Everyone ate until we were sick.

Carpenter's group hadn't came in yet and I had my shower taken before he got there. That gave me time to have my first bowel movement in four days, attempting to pass all those dry, undigested cornflake bars I ate. The jagged edges gave me the most painful five minutes I have ever had.

For the next three days we talked or vectored helicopters over our heads with hand radios, fired pyrotechnics, and took tests. During the eleventh day there, we were given the ground rules of the POW camp training, including lectures on how to act as POWs and how to get messages to fellow POWs. America's involvement in Vietnam had been going on for over ten years with many GIs, mostly fly boys, being captured. Each of us bought bracelets with the name of some POW written on it, made up by the wives of POWs in an effort to help us remember these men.

WE'RE ALL MAD, YOU KNOW

We ate a good meal that evening and I hid some tobacco and rolling papers on me before mustering at a staging area and waiting for the sun to go down. It had been down for thirty minutes with enough cloud cover to make the pasture ahead of us pitch black. We lined up along the length of the starting line for five hundred yards, and on signal, began crawling forward.

We crawled over flat land, feeling our way slowly for booby traps that criss-crossed the field. A ravine was in our way, followed by rows of concertina wire; rolled up barbed wire that until now I had only seen in movies. We crawled forward for close to a mile, taking several hours to cross. Near the end were some rolling hills, and although I was attempting to be careful, I tripped a wire that I noticed too late. A flare lit up my side of the hill like daylight and I found it impossible to hide from it. Had this been war, I would have been dead.

The flare burned for nearly ten minutes, as I waited for it to go out before continuing on. A few more flares went off across the field with enough light to cast a shadow even at my distance. Some holes were dug out of the ground beyond the hills and I rolled into one taking the opportunity to urinate after resting a moment. Another fifty yards and I crossed the last fence. Once there, I waited in a ditch for the enemy to find me.

I watched the instructor walk along the edge of the ditch until he came to me, telling me that I was a prisoner of war and to get up with my hands behind my neck. The instructor patted me down, yanked my arms down and put a burlap bag over my head. He grabbed me by the collar, led me forward for a couple hundred feet, told me not to move and left me alone.

I saw a light streaming through a hole in the sack and slowly worked the hole toward the front until I could see through it. Fourteen men were in line ahead of me. One at a time, people ahead of me were led to a small shack and taken inside. I didn't have to worry about what was going on inside for very long because my turn came quickly.

Once inside, the sack was stripped off my head. Two goons were standing beside me and a man was seated behind a desk. "How many men were in your squad?" He asked me bluntly.

"McGuire, Gary W. Airman, 446-48-8..." I responded in textbook Geneva Convention fashion, but was interrupted before I could finish.

"I don't give a damn who you are," he barked at me. "How many men were in your squad?"

I almost got my name out before one of the goons grabbed me by the arms and threw me up against a wall.

"How many?" the instructor demanded.

"McGuire, Gary,...."

"I'll have your fingers broken!" he screamed at me.

The two goons started for me and I believed for at least a second that they would really have broken my fingers, but before they could get to me, a man came in through a side door.

"Hold it!" he ordered as he walked over to me. He put his arm around my shoulders and walked me a few steps away from the goons telling me calmly, "I can only keep these guys off your back if you tell them what they want to know. Don't be a martyr for an unjust cause."

We stood there in silence as I wondered what to do. But there was really no choice as far as I was concerned. So I said, "McGuire, Gary W...."

"Get this man out of my sight!" the man screamed. The bag was put over my head and I was lead back outside.

The hole was no longer where I could see through it, but that didn't really matter. I felt like I was alone, even though I was in a line of other prisoners again. We stood there for close to an hour. The time was now close to 0200. A guard came by, took my hand and placed it on the shoulder of the man in front of me. We were lead another hundred yards to a damp, musty smelling room. The bag was removed, but the only thing I had time to see was the open cell in front of me before I was shoved inside and the door slammed behind me.

Enough light filtered in for my eyes to make out the wall and door, and a coffee can with one square of tissue in it. The doors stopped slamming closed and someone outside gave a speech, telling us that anyone caught sitting down on anything except our pot would be tortured. I wondered what they thought this was. I sat down in the darkness and silence helplessly waiting my turn. I could hear the guards opening and closing doors one at a time and getting closer. Two doors away, I stood up. When they got to me I was told to undress. I stood there naked as my clothes were searched, but my tobacco and papers went undetected. I sat back down and smiled to myself after getting dressed and locked inside my cell again. The smile didn't last too long however, as I felt a bowel movement coming on and cringed at the thought of eliminating into an open coffee can. I tightened my sphincter and concentrated on making the feeling pass, which worked for a while.

I'm sure I fell asleep, but a feeling I can't explain woke me up and I stood just as the door to my cell was being opened. They probably made some noise that my subconscious heard, but it seemed like ESP at the time. I was taken to a room and placed in an odd shaped box that was open at the top and side. They pushed me against the far wall, shoving the top down until my chin was only a few inches from my chest. The front pushed forward until my knees were also nearly in my chest. The side was slid in touching my side. The only things I could move were my fingers and toes. To a claustrophobic person this would have caused complete insanity. For anyone else, it created extreme discomfort as the muscles wanted to tighten and cramp. The process of talking to yourself mentally for self control is now called "bio-feedback." I only knew that panic was trying to set in and would have easily without talking myself out of it. Sensing time in dark, silent isolation is difficult, so I'm guessing that it was twenty minutes before they let me out.

Being squeezed up didn't help my elimination problem any. As bad as I hated to, I could hold it no more. Only an hour after getting out of the box, I defecated into my coffee can. This school was becoming an ordeal. One lousy square of the toilet tissue, hardly enough. It's said that you can always find something good in everything, in this case it's the fact that the olfactory becomes insensitive to a smell after a little while.

The hours passed and the silence was broken only by an occasional cough or a door being opened looking for people sitting down. When the doors were finally all opened, we took our coffee cans and disposed of them before being marched outside into the fresh, morning air. The little sleep I had gotten was showing in the way I felt, having spent most of the night awake and on my feet. And the interrogations were starting again.

When my time came to enter the room, I was unprepared for the screaming assault and badgering that came at me. When I refused to answer any questions with anything beside my name, rank, and serial number, a goon picked me up out of the chair I was sitting in, threw me to the floor and stated, "You have just been beaten severely!" I didn't know just what to do so the instructor called for an "Academic Situation."

When you are faced with torture," he told me, "ham it up a little. If you appear to endure pain they'll just torture you more, but if you appear in relentless agony, they may ease up a bit. Now return to your POW role."

I began screaming and rolling on the floor, praying that this never really happens to me. I thought about Lt. Rowe and all those that this really has happened to, making my anguish feel all the more real. The instructor thought I played the part well.

This went on until past noon and I was beginning to feel hungry again. We were marched a short distance to a genuine looking POW camp, complete with two chain link fences ten feet high with barbed wire at an angle on top. Between the two fences, German Shepherds patrolled. There were two elevated guard towers and only a few buildings. I wondered where they were going to put all of us.

WE'RE ALL MAD, YOU KNOW

Before we entered the gate, MacMahon was pulled out of formation and a machine gun was forced into his hands.

"Stand over by the gate as the prisoners pass through," he was ordered. Some people in civilian clothes were standing around by the gate. We were told they were the press and were there to take pictures. What a sickening feeling it must have been, having everyone in the world seeing him stand guard over his own men while a POW himself. He started doing stupid things with it, like dragging it around by the butt and dragging the barrel in the dirt. That got a guard in his face right away, but even so, when one photographer started to snap a picture, he turned the weapon up and looked down the barrel. He knew they wouldn't hand him a loaded gun but he worked the ejector just to make sure. They took the Thompson away from him after the press drove away and pushed him through the gate, locking it behind him.

We ended the march at some underground bunkers, tall enough to walk in if you were on your knees or bent way over at the waist. The floor was dirt but by then nobody cared. With ten people per hole, we were able to sit down for the first time in a while.

I thought this was as good a time as any for a smoke so I broke out my stash. The others in the hole couldn't believe I smuggled it in. I learned later that they were thinking it was a gift from our captors in return for information. Two prisoners were chosen to be informers, but it never dawned on them that gifts would have been too blatantly obvious.

121

Suspicion of me was growing as a half hour later the loudspeaker announced, "Airman McGuire, report to the commandants office."

"Why me?" I wondered as I slowly walked back to the office by the main gate.

A swing-out window was open, with a man sitting inside watching me walk up to him. I stood a few feet back from him saying only, "Airman McGuire reporting."

He just looked at me, not saying a word until he picked up a piece of pie and ate a bite. As he chewed on it my stomach growled.

"Would you like a bite?" he asked, offering the plate out the window.

One of our lessons said it was OK to accept food from the enemy as long as you haven't compromised yourself to get it. So I told him, "sure," and reached out for the plate.

He turned the plate upside down just as I almost had it and I watched the cream pie hit the dirt. I felt adrenaline rush through me and fixed him with a stare to maybe recognize him again someday. He saw the anger in my face and laughed for a minute. When that subsided his expression turned blank. He sat back and looked at me.

What in the hell is this all about? I wondered. It did have a purpose but it would be later before I found out what it was all about. The real informers were secretly talking to the camp commandant at the same time, but by announcing my name everyone assumed I was the informer.

Two other people's names were called as often as mine during the rest of the time there, giving them three decoys to cover their two informers. They had me sitting in a

WE'RE ALL MAD, YOU KNOW

room all alone, or standing outside the window never being asked a question. We had all been aroused from our caves after the first couple of hours. There was nothing to do after that, giving the PJs time to find each other. Carpenter believed that I wasn't talking to the enemy at first but after a while I think he doubted me. The camp commander had a small fire built and some guards brought in a large pot of what was supposed to be soup. It looked like dirty water with something floating in it and smelled of burnt egg shells. We ate our half bowl full anyway, wishing we could have some more.

Soon after chow we were taken to a classroom for re-education where the instructor explained the evils of capitalism and the virtues of communism. He tried to instigate a dialogue but no one would converse with him. A prisoner will never win an argument with his captors, and anything a POW says will be used against him. Time didn't allow us to become brainwashed, but the methods and techniques were obvious and would be difficult to endure over a long period without some signs of weakening.

We had been back outside after class for only a few minutes when a horn started blaring. One of the men had received an escape chit from the POW commander and sneaked away between some buildings as we left the class. He was by the fence under a guard tower, and hidden from the other tower by the buildings. I don't know how he intended to get out, but he never got through the first fence, tripping a wire that sounded the horn.

WE'RE ALL MAD, YOU KNOW

Only three escape attempts were permitted, being chosen by the POW commander and given a chit with a map, compass and some money. I went to see him later in the afternoon explaining what they were doing to me.

"If you'll give me a chit, the next time they call me in I can simply slip through a window and be long gone before they discover my absence."

"You just stay as far away from me as you can," he answered me coldly. It really made me angry, but there was nothing I could do. Everyone was convinced that I was the informer.

The other two escapees made it outside the fences somehow, but the cover of darkness was no help against the spotlights on the towers. The enemy, knowing what to expect in advance, didn't help their chances any either. The informers turned out to be two of the commander's most trusted men.

That night everyone had to stay outside and awake. We kept a small fire burning and took turns standing near it to shake the sleepiness and cold off a little. We ate another half bowl full of slimy soup, and I smoked my last cigarette in the open for all to see. I didn't care anymore that I had no friends. I knew I was no informer and that I had smuggled my smoke in. We could only watch the sky and wait for the sun to come up. Our second night without sleep, and it felt like it.

We watched as the sunrise began bringing color back to the landscape, but we were herded back into our holes before the first rays of light broke the horizon. As sleep tried to overcome me, I heard three names being called to report to the commandant. Mine was one.

WE'RE ALL MAD, YOU KNOW

The three of us entered the commandant's office and were offered a chair at a desk across from the commandant. Four guards were close by for his safety, but we were close enough that I decided, if it came to it, I could jump across the table and stick my finger through the soft spot in his throat and pull out his trachea before the guards killed me.

"You three have been chosen to be repatriated as a gesture of our good will toward all American people," the commandant said pleasantly with a smile. "All you need to do is sign the form in front of you, and you will be flown home. Your loving families are waiting for you."

I didn't see any reason not to believe him, but asked if I could read the document first.

"Sure, sure," he replied. But I didn't have time to get past the first paragraph before his true colors showed. He retorted impatiently, "I don't have all day. Either sign the paper and go home or go back to your hole and die there!"

My choices seemed limited and it did say I was not guilty of any war crimes so, like the other two had already done, I signed the paper.

"Good," he said, "very good. You will return to your hole now. We will notify you when your transportation arrives."

I knew as I walked back that I'd regret signing that document. I took a seat back in my hole wishing I had a smoke. Hardly ten minutes went by before the announcement came for all POWs to report at the speakers podium. As I walked over with the group in my hole, I was taken by two guards to stand at the far back of the formation with the two other repatriated GIs. The other

POWs fell in at attention according to rank, putting the PJs in the last row with their backs to me, not more than fifteen yards in front of me.

The camp commandant, in real life a USAF full bird colonel, came out of his office and walked briskly across the compound to the elevated platform. He looked briefly at the crowd, then focused his attention on the three of us.

"Three of your fellow prisoners," he began slowly, "have signed statements acknowledging their part in the heinous war crimes..."

"Oh shit," I said under my breath as he continued, ."..committed against the innocent victims of capitalist aggression."

"Damn, damn, damn," I muttered to myself. It was the old get their signature and forge it on any paper they want to trick. These people have been pissing me off regular and I couldn't hold the adrenaline back any longer without doing something. "You can tear my paper up." I said but not loud enough to be heard over the speech still coming from the commandant.

."..so in response to this gross inequity of justice, they have voluntarily surrendered their citizenship to the United States."

At this point my life meant absolutely nothing to me. My instincts told me to take a couple of steps forward. I said in a voice loud enough for everyone to hear, "You can stick that paper clean up your ass!"

I had just enough time to see every head in the place turn toward me before a giant of a man grabbed me from behind. He picked me straight up about seven feet, turned me on my back and slammed me to the ground. Almost

126

immediately, he jerked me off the ground and I landed on my feet. As I was coming up, I had my hand clenched in a tight fist and was looking at the spot on his throat where I intended to cut this big man down. Some movement in the crowd caught my attention. It was all the PJs moving at once in our direction.

I looked back at the guard holding me. He held me still at arms length, giving me a look that questioned what I was going to do. We glared at each other for a moment and I realized that it could end now, or get bloody.

I relaxed my posture. This was, after all, only pretend. The guard, wanting to be sure that he got the last word in, put a finger in my face and said, "You're dead!"

The PJs had stopped about five yards short, seeing that the incident didn't escalate. We heard the gate being opened and the commandant declared this exercise to be concluded. A sergeant hustled up to me saying, "You should go right now and apologize to the colonel."

"Do I have something to apologize for?" I asked him back.

"You told a colonel to stick something up his ass. Yes. I'd say you do."

I made my way over to the colonel. "I didn't mean anything personal by my remark," I explained.

The colonel nodded his head toward the front gate saying, "Forget it."

I walked away without saluting. Carpenter and some others waited up for me to see if anything else would happen to me.

"What would you guys have done if we'd started slinging fists?" I asked him.

"We were going to try to keep that gorilla from killing
you," Carpenter said, laughing.
We made our way slowly back to the chow hall located
about a mile away. As sleepy as everyone was, sleep would
have to wait for a steak and egg breakfast and a shower.
Then we slept for twelve straight hours.
We just managed to eat before making assembly at
noon. This was to be our final de-briefing, us PJ's sitting
off to the right of the main body of students. The colonel
came out to give us our evaluation. He said our overall
performance was good, emphasizing how easy it is to trust
your enemy and abandon your friends.
."..and one man deserves special recognition for
courage and self-control. Airman Gary McGuire."
If that didn't surprise me enough, the entire class arose
to their feet applauding for what was my first, and
probably only, standing ovation.

Chapter Seven

Pararescue Transition School

We stayed the night partying with the three guys we knew as both friends and instructors. The parting the next morning was nearly unbearable. They wanted to go with us.

It was the 25th day of July when we boarded a plane in Spokane to take us on the final leg of the journey. We landed in Salt Lake City early that Wednesday afternoon, calling for base transportation to come get us one last time. Hill AFB was twenty miles north of Salt Lake City and ten miles South of Ogden, with an Ogden mailing address. Three miles to the east rose the western edge of the Rocky Mountains.

129

We had had it so easy for the past forty-five days that we questioned the shape we were in. As we entered the main gate we felt the familiar sensation of fear of the unknown. What were they going to do to us here? Whatever it was, we knew that they had only two months to do it in. We should have been more scared than we were.

The bus stopped out front of another WWII barracks. The only person to meet us was the squadron's first sergeant. He told us the class ahead of us was in helicopter school, and that we could have the barracks when they moved out. He pointed to a much older barracks behind us saying, "Find yourselves a bunk upstairs."

Fred Scantling and another airman set back from the class ahead of us were in the open bay, leaving only three to graduate from the original eight that left Lackland six weeks before we did. We were also joined by a reserve PJ sergeant catching up with advancements in training.

We were still unpacking in the upstairs bay when Setchfield looked through the window and spotted three PJs walking toward the barracks. They had lots of stripes on their arms and looked as mean as we expected them to. We hustled over to stand in front of our lockers, waiting for them to finish walking up the stairs.

They stood in the doorway looking at us for a moment as we stood at attention.

"Drop!" the sergeant yelled.

Without giving us a second to recover he ordered, "Drop!" again. It had been a long time but I had not lost as much strength as I thought. We remained in the learning rest while he talked to us.

130

WE'RE ALL MAD, YOU KNOW

"You are at the 1550th Student Squadron, Air Training Wing, Hill AFB, Utah. I'm Sergeant Cooper, these are sergeants Fisk and Crall. You'll meet sergeants Scott and O'Neal later. While you are here, you will be expected to display exemplary behavior. You will pay close attention to everything you are taught and obey every order. You have one hour to have this place squared away, then fall out for PT."

We didn't talk at all as we quickly unpacked, made bunks and shined everything in sight. As we fell out for PT, our guts rolled and churned. We still weren't talking.

PT was no harder than it had been at Lackland. We thanked God for that, but it still wasn't easy. We were just tough. Cooper wasn't impressed. Hell, nothing we ever did impressed these instructors. They smiled only when they thought someone might quit.

Cooper followed us back to the barracks where we were given some information about Mountain School, our first phase of training.

"You are the luckiest people in the world," Cooper began in typical GI voice. "Everyone else that wants to learn mountain climbing must spend thousands of dollars at the Sierra Club. You're not only getting it for free, you're getting paid for it. So we expect you to learn it well. In the next two weeks, you'll be able to tie twenty-two different knots, rappel, belay and climb, or you'll be out." He looked at us for a long moment. "Class starts tomorrow morning."

The class was held in the barracks. Patiently, each knot was detailed. Three rules applied to every knot: the short end always had to be four inches long, loops had to be six inches tall and there was a time limit placed on tying each knot, depending on the degree of difficulty, ranging from ten to thirty seconds. We were tested each morning for three days. Anyone failing even one knot on the third test was out. "Remember," we were warned, "tying the knot is not good enough."

Each morning we boarded the back of a duce-and-a-half truck that took us to a thirty foot tall tower. The mouth of a mountain pass opened up only a mile east, and every morning a cold thirty mph wind blew down the pass into our faces. We wouldn't climb the tower yet, as we had to pass the knot test first and learn to fall off a mountain.

Everyone failed the first knot test. I wondered if it was possible to fail the "falling off a mountain" test.

To practice, one man would tie a four coil bowline (pronounced "bowlin") around their waist from one end of a hundred foot rope or mountain coil. Another man, anchored to the ground, held the other end on belay, with the coil going around his back and held against his chest with his right hand. The left hand was used only as a guide. We took off in a dead run, the rope uncoiling behind us.

The coil stretched tight in the middle of my stride. My legs, arms and head continued forward as my waist was snapped back. Arms and legs whipped back and I landed flat on my back. I rolled over on my knees trying to catch my breath.

"On your feet!" was the order.

We dragged ourselves up and changed places with our belay man. He didn't have it much easier. As the belay man, I held the brake hard against my chest watching the coil unwind to its end. I felt the rope burn against my back as it stretched against the force pulling on it. The rope anchoring me tugged hard into my stomach.

"Ouch!" McLafferty yelled out in pain. He opened his left hand and blood ran down his arm. He had gripped the rope with his guide hand instead of his brake hand. Loose skin flapped on both sides of the friction burn on his palm. We all thought he was through, but he had come too far to lose now. He took off his fatigue top and wrapped his hand in his T-shirt. He was told he could go on if he could, but would receive no special consideration.

We were back on base for a late lunch, practiced our knots, then went to PT. We took long hot showers and nursed our wounds.

Most passed the second knot test. We built rope bridges and practiced falling off the mountain. I had failed the first two knot tests, so the pressure to pass the final test was tremendous. To fail this test didn't mean that I would be set back, it meant I was out! The trick was knowing where to start the knot in order to finish with the right length of loop and tail. I worked more carefully than I ever had, thinking ahead with every bend. Finally I succeeded. I breathed a massive sigh of relief, but Cooper seemed truely disappointed that we all passed the final test.

After the last knot test, we went to the tower which had two lanes. Setchfield and MacMahon were first to fall. They and their two belay men climbed the ladder to the top. Two instructors were waiting there.

"Your instruction is over," they had just told us. "On this tower our only responsibility is to keep you from killing yourself when you do something stupid." They watched closely, but rarely spoke.

Both the climber and belay man double checked the anchor, snap links and knots. The climbers scaled down the face of the tower about ten feet and were ordered to stop. They gripped the wall, calling for slack. They pulled enough slack to allow the bottom of the loop to reach their feet. If we were to ever fall, we were to shout the word "falling." This lets the belay man know to expect a jerk.

They pushed themselves away from the wall. It's surprising how much speed and momentum you generate from a seven foot fall. The coil does stretch, but the stop is sudden enough that an "ugh" came out of them as their backs arched just before slamming up against the wall. A high pitched "Setchfield OK" brought a chuckle out of us, but was restrained knowing it would soon be our turn. MacMahon's feet somehow swung upward, turning him upside down. He slammed against his back. We each got to fall and be on belay twice.

At the barracks that night we compared the degrees of our injuries. After five days of rope burns, McLafferty was beaten up the most. His hand looked awful. We all had bruised imprints of mountain coil across our backs, arms and waist. We ached everywhere, but the worst was over.

Rappelling, as easy and fun as it is, is deadly if done wrong. I put the rope in my snap link backward, using two loops of rope behind the snap link instead of from the rope in front of it. I turned backward and stepped to the edge of the tower. "McGuire on rap...", I started saying.

"Stand by," the instructor interrupted calmly. "Step forward away from the edge."

WE'RE ALL MAD, YOU KNOW

I stepped forward. He pulled on the rope. The snap link flipped over, putting the loops on top of the snap links gate. My eyes widened as the snap link opened, allowing the coils to slip out. "You owe me a bottle of Chivas Regal," the instructor declared. That was the standard charge for saving a students life.

The climbing phase of transition school included a walk much like the one at survival school. We were trucked into the Rockies and dropped off in a field at about six thousand feet elevation. Each team had two men except mine, which had three. One of the "set backs" was with me and Steve Birkland.

We were to reach the saddle of two mountain peaks by the following afternoon after climbing to nearly ten thousand feet. Before noon of the second day, our third member refused to climb any higher. Birkland and I had to change directions to make the climb easier to keep the team together. Although it was now mostly downhill, it was thick with underbrush and fallen trees.

From the instructors vantage point at the saddle, they could see us coming a half mile away. We didn't see them until we got to within a hundred yards of them. "You guys couldn't sneak up on a rock," Fisk said in disgust. "Look behind you."

The other teams were in plain view and could have been easily picked off.

We climbed up and rappelled down the tower one more day mostly in teams with one of us in a stretcher. The following day we boarded a Super Jolly Green Helicopter with all our climbing equipment, field equipment and rations for five days in an accompanying Jolly Green. We flew south west of Salt Lake City for forty-five minutes towards a remote range of rocks in the Wasatch Mountains. All the techniques we learned at the tower were repeated here except, falling off the mountain. If that happened, it would be real. There were four climbing lanes, each progressively harder.

The first three days were a piece of cake. The climbing lanes were preset with pitons and about sixty feet high. The first two sloped in a bit. The third lane was straight up. The last lane began straight up the first fifteen feet, then bent outward and turned flat so we were climbing across the bottom of this rock ledge for another ten feet before we went up over the ledge. No amount of PT ever caused more exhausted, twitching muscles or created more sweat than this.

Our rope bridge was built over a stream. As we crawled across it, the instructor would say, "and the winds came!", and begin swinging the rope. He wouldn't stop until we fell. The water felt icy cold.

Our last day out was supposed to be easy. All we had to do was walk to the top of the mountain. No climbing gear would be required but we would have to spend the night there, so we carried all our field equipment.

The fact was, if we left camp at 0600 and humped our butts hard, we might get to the top before sundown. We were allowed only one canteen of water. It wasn't enough. There was not a path. If you didn't like the way the man ahead of you went, you were to go a different way.

WE'RE ALL MAD, YOU KNOW

Phil Parker, early on, went what he thought was a better way. It was easy at first, but I didn't trust the part we couldn't see ahead. I traversed back toward a ridge and could see that Phil was getting himself in trouble. The ledge his feet were on was narrowing sharply. The corner we couldn't see around was not passable and he couldn't get back around the bend. His hands were tiring and he had no way to rest them. On the ledge above him, Fisk was watching. "Can't get back the way you came, huh?" Fisk noted.

"I think my hands are slipping!" Parker said earnestly.

Fisk looked over across the ravine where Cooper was sitting on a rock watching. "He says he's slipping," Fisk yelled.

Cooper pulled his sunglasses off, looked a moment, put his glasses back on and yelled back, "Yeah, I think he's right."

Parker was near panic and exhausted. His hands slipped and he began slapping at the rock trying to find a hand hold as gravity pulled him backward. Fisk's hand grabbed Parkers wrist and with shear strength and probably some adrenaline, pulled Parker, one hundred seventy pounds without the field gear, up and over the ledge, standing him on his feet. "You owe me a bottle of Chives Regal," were the only words said.

We used every free climbing technique known. Phil's fall would have been more than thirty feet. Many places could have topped ninety. A solid rock slope we traversed was so steep and slick, a man slid twenty seconds or so before crashing into the corner of some rocks. He was the same set back that refused to climb higher on the mountain walk with Birkland and me. He was crying, saying that he couldn't go on. It was his last chance. We climbed on.

The view was getting better by the foot, but the water was running out and we were a long way from the top. Each horizon loomed higher than the last with a twenty foot chimney climb just ahead. I was tired as I started, but found myself exhausted two- thirds of the way up. Determination and fear are strong motivators. As my hands reached the top I allowed my legs to rest. The relief was bliss. Just that moment of rest gave me enough strength to pull myself over the edge and I rolled over on my stomach.

"Move out, McGuire," the order came almost sympathetically. I went to my knees first, then struggled to my feet, waking away in a stumble. It was time for my last swallow of water. The sun was hours from going down. That was the last hard climb. The rest of the way was easy enough but water was what we really wanted.

Parker stopped on a rock to rest with Carpenter and a couple of us caught up. We sat there looking out over a vast area of southern Utah. The sun was getting lower all the time. In the cracks of the rocks stood some water. Green stuff was floating in it and bugs skimmed its surface.

"Ever drink panther piss?" Parker asked. He bent over, pushed the stuff off the top and took a drink. We waited a moment and when he didn't die we decided to take a drink. It was better than a parched throat.

Our legs felt like rubber as we stood to continue. Each step was up hill but we figured it couldn't be much further.

It was. The sun was down and it was getting dark when we reached the top. I finished pitching my tent just as darkness set in. I ate some rations, got a canteen of water from an instructor and fell square to sleep.

We packed that morning and made our way down along a much easier side of the mountain. We came to a road where two trucks were waiting for us and our gear. It was a five hour ride back to the base.

The class ahead of us was gone, allowing us to move from the open bay to slightly newer barracks, which gave us each our own room. We also had some weekends off and some money, since we hadn't been anywhere we could spend any for a long time. Parker, McLafferty and I bought motorcycles to ride through the mountains.

During one of our weekend excursions I got a little cocky and began rounding curves at forty plus mph, and the inevitable happened. One curve was sharper than expected, loose gravel and oil was thicker than usual, and a sheer drop loomed just off the shoulder. The bike was leaning into the turn as far as possible and I was off the throttle, but still, centrifugal force was winning and I was about to become airborne on a Honda. Either I laid the bike over or it just slipped out from under me, but either way I hit hard enough to bounce both myself and the bike up on it's wheels again. I kept moving and did a somersault over the handle bars. I landed on my back in front of the bike and the damn thing did the same thing right over the top of me. It landed off to one side and we both slid, tumbling and rolling to a stop only inches from the drop off.

I didn't hurt anywhere. Blood was oozing from my wrist and I felt myself stiffening up. My knees and elbows had lost some skin as well. I stood up and took off my helmet. A crack ran the length from between my eyes to the back of my neck. No bones were broken. Even my bike started once I stood it up. We had been warned not to get hurt doing something stupid, so I told them that I tripped over a curb while going out for a pass while playing football. "You must have been running thirty-five miles an hour when you," the instructor paused before ending with, "tripped over that curb." Of course he knew I was lying, but then, he knew I couldn't tell him the truth.

There was one other time I got hurt off base. Six of us had gone to McDonalds for dinner in Ogden. Parker and Setchfield were outside when three pick up trucks full of high school kids rolled in. Their football team had just lost a game.

Four of them came up to Parker. From the window I couldn't hear, but I could see Parker shaking his head saying something like, 'you really don't want to do this.' I was walking toward the door as I said to the girl behind me to call the police. At that moment one guy swung at Parker but missed. Parker's reflexes were fast and he came up from the dodge swinging. Before I reached the door another dude standing by a truck pulled out a baseball bat, tagging Parker up side the head from his blind side. He fell to the ground, out cold. Yet another standing near kicked him in the face. At that time I arrived, getting in only one solid punch before nine of them were on top of me. Setchfield had five or more on him since the first swing. The other three PJs were swarmed as well.

Setchfield was first to beat off his gang. He said he saw three crowds beating in toward a center, with a fist

140

emerging from the center in what seemed to be something right out of a cartoon.

I don't really remember getting hit, but I was bruised all over my back. I could only duck my head and sling my arms in a round house fashion in all directions as hard and fast as I could. I must have thumped on a few because it wasn't long before they scattered as fast as they had jumped. It happened so fast they were able to jump into their trucks and speed away before the police arrived.

Parker recovered with no worse than a chipped tooth.

The instructors laughed at us saying, "What a bunch of pussies you guys are, letting a couple of high school boys whip your asses." It did seem like we spent a lot of time licking our wounds.

Our next training segment was Advanced Medical Training. We were tested the first morning to see how much we had forgotten. Having done better then expected, we spent only three days going over our weak spots. We bandaged, splinted and did a lot of CPR. By Friday evening we were starting IVs on each other and putting naso-gastric tubes up each others noses.

We devoted a good deal of time memorizing the contents of our medical jump kits. Each item had its own location and had to be packed and folded snugly for the flaps to close. It was tight. We carried two controlled substances. Demerol and amphetamines. They were signed in and out each time the crews changed. As you probably guessed, the Demerol was for the patient, the amphetamines were for the PJ. "You had better have one damn good reason should you ever take one," we were sternly cautioned.

The Air Force is extremely particular about who they let near their aircraft. Never knowing just when a solid, sane man might crack, every crew member is required to see the psychiatrist once a year. As I stepped inside the office, I was wondering if my answers to his questions were going to be what he wanted to hear.

"Did you live a happy childhood?"

"Yes," I answered. Surprised at the simplicity of the question.

"Gary," he began very seriously, "do you ever talk to yourself?" I started to say no but then it seemed harmless enough so I confessed, "Yes, once in a while."

"Tell me then Gary, do you ever answer yourself?"

I felt myself feeling uneasy not knowing what my answer was going to mean to him. "Yes, I suppose sometimes I do." He looked at his paper as he wrote his notes. He looked up over the rim of his glasses. "Well then Gary," he said as if he questioned my sanity, "do you ever say 'huh'?"

"No," I answered, thinking he was the one who was crazy.

"Well hell," he said, "you're as sane as anybody I've ever met. Go on, get out of my office."

We knew something different was coming up when Monday morning started out with a secured briefing, complete with MP's outside guarding the windows and doors. We were reminded of the penalties under the

WE'RE ALL MAD, YOU KNOW

Uniformed Code of Military Justice regarding the divulging of secret military information. The secret was, we would be using live goats for practice. What was funny was, it wasn't the Russians that we were keeping the secret from. It was the Mormons. They would never accept the use of live animals for medical practice. America was at war and we could find ourselves there in a few months. One fact of war is that men get shot and blown up. We needed hands-on experience in a controlled environment if we hoped to do anyone any good under fire. We felt the end justified the means. For the next two days we would study anatomy, cricothyroidotomy, eviscerations, burns, fractures, etc. and on Thursday we would go to the infamous "goat lab."

Our instructor was one of only five PJ officers in the USAF and all five were permanently stationed at the Pentagon. He was a major with an unexpectedly pleasant personality. He told us Wednesday afternoon to report to the goat lab no later than 0500 the next morning. A truck would be waiting for us.

The truck was there when we arrived. Eight goats were unloaded into a small room off to the side of the lab. The major injected each of them with fifty milligrams of Demerol and we waited for the animals to calm down.

Two men were assigned per goat. The goats were relaxed enough that they put up little resistance when we shaved their hair off. Each team had their own table. After the animals were anesthetized to ensure they would feel no pain, the major would go around the tables breaking their legs, cutting arteries, slicing abdomens and committing other mayhem. After four hours of concentrated effort in splinting broken bones, stopping bleeding, and other medical care, the animals were given a lethal injection. We then did an autopsy to identify the internal organs. The animals were then bagged and reloaded in the truck to be taken away for disposal. A few years later an animal rights group raised a massive media fuss regarding "Goat Lab" practices and the military was forced to close down this segment of instruction. I felt it was a massive injustice to have our first "patients" be human beings on actual rescue missions instead of goats. But the animal "rights" people obviously didn't feel the same way.

We all passed the final written test with high marks and said good-bye to the major. Finally, we were getting back off the ground. The ARRS had four aircraft at their disposal. The C-130 Hercules, the HH-53 Super Jolly Green Giant, the HH-3 Jolly Green and the UH-1N Huey. We were only going to be certified on the C-130 for now.

Having been here for nearly a month, and living in the newer barracks, we were finally feeling more comfortable. The instructors could sense our relaxed posture and reminded us often that we weren't PJs yet, and the quit sheet was always nearby.

Apparently, somebody in our group didn't take this warning seriously enough and became a little lax in his discipline. I don't remember who did what, but it must have been something really stupid because the reprisal was severe. I think some dust was found in the barracks during inspection one morning. Even though our training was nearing an end, the routine of spit shine, PT, and "drop" went on constantly.

For this infraction we were loaded in trucks and driven to the tower area. A second truck followed. There was a dusty pit that we used to build our rope bridges over. As we stood in single file behind the second truck, which contained six fifty-five gallon drums of water, the instructor scooped five gallons out and poured it over Carpenters head. He was ordered to low crawl through the pit and back to the truck. Each of us in turn received our bucket of water on the head and ordered to follow right on Carpenter's heels.

"Kick up more dirt!" they ordered. "Move your asses, you're going too slow. Tighten it up. Get you faces closer to the heals of the man in front of you. We want to see mud on your faces," they yelled. "Don't miss a stride, keep moving."

It was over a hundred yards round trip, dragging pounds of mud inside our shirts and pants. Our eyes squinted to avoid the larger chunks being thrown and kicked in our faces. The moment of rest we got as the next bucket of water drenched us only helped a moment. Carpenter was held up to go last to get dirt and mud in his face, too. On the fourth trip I realized this would be a marathon, and it was. It went on until they ran out of water. We were dragging our asses, flopping our arms and legs in exhausted agony. Our lungs burned.

"Fall in," barked an order. "Drop!"

We couldn't even do the required thirty six push ups. We fell out of unison early and used the leaning rest often.

145

Quit sheets were stuck under our faces. "Sign the damn thing McGuire!" was shouted in my face.

"No sergeant," I replied loudly.

Hell, I was in the leaning rest, but I kept that thought to myself. Each of us was assured how unwelcome we were and that Pararescue would be better off without us. In the end, they didn't get any signatures and we were driven back to the barracks.

As we crawled out of the back of the truck, we saw six new arrivals watching us. They seemed mesmerized by our appearance.

"Tomorrow morning this pig sty you live in better shine or I'll have your asses back in that pit. Do you hear me?"

"Yes sergeant!" we yelled in unison.

"Drop!" he roared back, and walked away as we counted them out. The six new boys dropped as well.

We didn't see much of them as they started mountain school the next day. Not one of us got any sleep that night as we shined and polished every surface in the whole place. I had thrown my muddy fatigues out the door early in the evening and remembered them at about 0430 that morning. I decided to hide them under the barracks. The only access was under the front porch so I threw them as far under as possible.

At 0800, we were ready. Three instructors spent ten minutes in each room. We only dropped a few times as no matter how hard they looked, everything was in perfect order. It was mid September and the sun was coming up later all the time. Two other instructors showed up and waited outside for the inspection to finish. I could see them from the corner of my eye as I stood at attention in the hall

146

outside my room. They leaned against the stair rail talking. One instructor rested his boot on the first stair and looked inside the building. At that moment, the suns rays lined up perfectly to shine through the steps and on to my uniform. The inspection had just ended and the three inspectors walked past me toward the front porch.

My uniform. I saw the instructor who spotted it cock his head to one side. He didn't know yet just what he had found. My heart pounded in my chest as he reached under the stairs.

"McGuire!" my name thundered from his mouth. "Front and center!"

"Just what in the hell are your dirty fatigues doing under my porch?" he demanded instantly upon my arrival.

"I didn't know what else to do with them, sergeant," was my feeble reply.

"Get'em out here Carpenter!" he yelled at the Barracks.

The thunder of jump boots just preceded the team as they hustled outside. "Fall in!" came the next order. I joined them in formation.

"McGuire, get your face on the ground and eat some grass. You so much as glance up and you're out. You got that?"

"Yes, sergeant," I submitted.

"Now it's up to your team. You disgraced them. Let them decide if you stay or go. It will only take one vote. Who says McGuire goes?"

A long moment passed. Carpenter once wanted me out so bad he prayed for a chance like this. My future was being decided right now.

"On your feet McGuire."

I jumped to attention.

No one moved. The instructor was slow to speak.

"The team says you can stay," he said brutally. "Get'em to class, Carpenter." I noticed I was breathing again. I didn't say thank you. They didn't expect me to. I looked at Carpenter but he just said, "Fall in McGuire" and led us off to class double-time as we sang about how much we liked it here.

Having passed the written C-130 test, we were ready to enter the jump phase. We spent two days going back through the techniques we learned at Ft. Benning. We were also issued the wet suits that we had been measured for back at Lackland some six months earlier.

Unlike the Army that drops hundreds of men at once, we operated in two man teams. If you weren't on the first team out, you got to ride around. The last team out rode a lot. The first two jumps were daytime land jumps to familiarize us with the equipment and procedures again, not to mention the anticipation, fear and smell of JP-4 jet fuel.

The third jump was to be at night. The lights in the cabin were red to aid in our night vision, and everything was a "go" for the jump. Two instructors went first. The next team stood up for their equipment check, hooked up and got as far as standing in the door when the safety man put his arm across the jumpers chest and eased them back from the door. One of the instructors had broken his ankle after landing on a rock. The jump was canceled and rescheduled.

We flew to Portland, Oregon for the next jump. The trees there were tall enough and thick enough for a good chance to get a hang-up. During the demonstration of the "tree jump suite", the instructor showed us why we should double check the radial crotch strap. He kicked his assistant square in the crotch hard enough to raise him off the ground. Should you straddle a limb while crashing through the trees, this radial strap saved the family jewels. Our helmets had plastic bubbles to protect our faces.

Parker was my partner, jumping from the right door. The left door jumper always goes first. After exiting the aircraft, I made a left turn toward the target. Parker was a good thirty-five pounds heavier than me, dropping under, and behind me and going in the opposite direction.

"Phil," I yelled. "The target's this way!"

Over a hundred yards separated us as he yelled back, "The trees are taller this way."

They weren't that much taller, and I could see the "bullseye" on the target zone if I stayed on my course. To change direction now would put me down in the youngest growth of trees.

Getting hung up in a tree is not as easy as it sounds. I crashed through limb after limb, falling hard to the ground as my 'chute slid off the side of the tree.

Cooper was glaring at me as I walked up carrying my spent parachute. "Where's your partner?"

"Last I saw of him, he turned upwind. He's out there somewhere."

"Just what in the hell are you doing here with your partner still out there?" he screamed. "Never leave your partner! What if he's out there hurt? You go where he goes! Now find him!"

149

WE'RE ALL MAD, YOU KNOW

It didn't take long to locate Phil, and everyone else. And out of the whole drop, only one man got a good hang-up, allowing him to rapell down the way we practiced so many times prior to the actual jump.

We stayed in the Pink Flamingo Motel that night. The first civilian lifestyle we had experienced in so long we didn't know how to act. We got moderately drunk, laughing about our screw-ups and what they might do to us next.

"Next" turned out to be the Scuba Jump Phase.

This was the last big hurdle. More trainees were washed out here than anywhere since Lackland. We had less than two weeks left to complete three daytime and two night SCUBA jumps. If you hit the door once, you were sent back to the beginning of transition school. Hit the door the second time through, or any minor infraction and you were out. Hitting the door has always been hard to prevent. Now came the added weight of dual 40 cubic foot SCUBA tanks to the main and reserve parachutes, med kit, life raft and other sundry equipment on your back, while jumping into a 140 mph wind far enough to clear the parachute from the edge of the door before the prop blast throws you back. At best, you clear the door by only a few inches. At worst, you bounce along the side of the aircraft, spinning as the parachute deploys, the suspension lines twisting, preventing the chute from catching air. It doesn't get much worse. We jumped with our swim fins on, strapped to our ankles so they wouldn't come off. They would flap wildly as we stood in the door ready to jump, adding to the difficulty of clearing the door.

150

WE'RE ALL MAD, YOU KNOW

We jumped into Utah lake. Although it was fresh water, it would prove years later to be the most polluted body of water in the Western United States. After splashing down, a waiting boat would pick up our parachutes but not us. We inflated our rafts and pushed and pulled them well over a mile to shore. There, as in all of our landings, we faced mock injuries to treat and evacuate.

McLafferty and I were paired up for our first night SCUBA jump. We differed, gear and all, by only a few pounds. I was in the left door, McLafferty was in the right. His safety man was to slap him on the thigh a full second after the jumpmaster slapped me, to stagger us slightly. The slaps were nearly instantaneous, resulting in our exiting the aircraft at the same time. Once under our canopies, he turned right toward the target as I turned left.

"Look out!" McLafferty yelled. But it was too late. Our parachutes collided and we swung past each other screaming. The pendulum effect swung us back and away from each other.

"That was pretty close," I said over my shoulder. I turned right, then left. He turned left, then right. We did it again.

"Okay, McGuire, you go first."

I pulled both toggles, dumping air to fall below McLafferty before releasing the left toggle to turn back toward the target. By then we had lost so much altitude that we landed far short.

"What were you guys doing up there, disco dancing?" Cooper asked while I was still in the water. He had no problem watching our gyrations, illuminated in the bright bursts of the strobe lights we carried.

WE'RE ALL MAD, YOU KNOW

On our last nighttime SCUBA jump, I wrapped some tobacco and papers up water tight and placed them inside my wetsuit along with some highly water-resistant matches. Once in the water, I swam over to meet Fred and there, in the middle of Utah lake in the black of the night, we enjoyed a smoke.

It was early October. Graduation was only a few days away and only one SCUBA jump left. Our hearts dropped when we learned that Steve Birkland, nearly 300 pounds of solid muscle, and probably the largest man ever to train this hard, hit the damn door.

"Don't worry about me," he told us. "This has been so much fun, I'm looking forward to going through it again."

He eventually made it.

Graduation day was anti-climatic. But I will never forget the feeling of accomplishment and pride I felt each time I stepped outside and put on my maroon beret.

Chapter Eight

Helicopter School

Snow had been capping the mountains since the week before graduation, and with each rain the snow line crept down hill. We had one month of flights, debriefings and class work ahead of us but at least now we were PJs. No more inspections. We wouldn't hear "drop" anymore. If we went some place, we could actually walk. We went from the lowest form of life on earth to equals with the men who, only a few days ago, hated us for invading their private domain. It was an uneasy peace, but peace just the same.

The class work was brief, as we were expected to study from the operations manual and a pocket book of checklists. Nothing in the Air Force was ever left to chance or guess work. The first concern, always, is safety; being professional in our work and not doing anything stupid.

We were issued flight suits, (a pair of overalls made with flame retarding material and more pockets than I can remember), gloves, sunglasses and a switch blade knife. The flight helmet was the most individual aspect of our flight gear. Each helmet lining was form fitted to the wearer's head and it's comfort was surprising.

Another aircraft was added to our list of those we qualified on as crew members, the HH-53 Super Jolly Green Giant. A huge helicopter, it has five rotors, two jet engines and enough room inside to carry eleven stretchers. There were three 53s for our flights, but usually only two were airworthy at any given time. Two were silver and one camouflage, but all rescue aircraft had one thing in common; a yellow pair of stripes near the tail and the word "rescue" between them. At the right crew entrance, just behind and below the right engine was mounted the motor for the rescue hoist, which basically, was a hook on the end of a two hundred-fifty foot cable with several attachments. The controls were operated from just inside the door with the right hand. The left hand steadied the cable.

Each flight consisted of the pilot, co-pilot, flight mechanic engineer, two PJs and an instructor PJ. We had morning, afternoon and night flights with 24 hour crew rest prior to each flight. Because of this schedule, even though we lived in the same barracks, we didn't see much of each other. One training flight, however, did put four of us together. On that flight we fired the mini-gun, a scaled down version of the multi-barreled Vulcan cannon. In

WE'RE ALL MAD, YOU KNOW

Vietnam, C-47 cargo transports had been converted into gunships mounting Vulcan cannons, and were affectionately called Puff the Magic Dragon. The Vulcan spits out six thousand rounds per minute. The mini-gun could only deliver four thousand. That's still an incredible sixty-six rounds per second. It was powered by two 12 volt batteries that spun the barrels, synchronizing each round to load, fire, and eject. To that end, two triggers were required. The left trigger was squeezed first, instantly firing at two thousand rounds-per-minute. Then, if desired, the right trigger could be pulled delivering an additional two thousand rpm. To cease fire, the right trigger must be released first to slow it down, then the left trigger was released to stop it. To do it differently would cause the gun to jam, requiring that it be disassembled. Not a good thing to happen in a tight spot when all firepower was required to cover a rescue in a hostile area.

Four thousand rounds-per-minute consumes ammo so fast that you really only wanted to use it in a panic situation, but it's impressive. The barrels spin so fast they're a blur. Fire is exploding three-feet out of the barrel in a solid flame. The sound, muffled by ear plugs and flight helmet, reminded me of the buzz of a bumble bee. Every fifth round was a tracer, and from one thousand feet, at a forty-five degree angle, there is a solid red line from the gun to the ground. My mother couldn't miss with this thing. It's like spraying the ground with a garden hose. Everything gets hit.

A few C-130s were also equipped with the Vulcan cannon and a 105mm howitzer. The cannon was aimed by laser, and when it fired, the aircraft was reputed to buck to the right about a hundred yards. This aircraft, known as "Spectre," was classified Top Secret, and when one was shot down, it was promptly destroyed to prevent the technology from falling into enemy hands.

Most of the four-hour flights were devoted to the pilots. They practiced approaches, emergency procedures, and did lots of autorotations; that is, they would simulate engine loss by cutting the power and lowering the collective stick to reduce blade pitch. The machine feels like it drops like a rock, but actually is in a controlled glide. The air passing through the rotors spins them just fast enough so that if the pilot flares the aircraft at just the right height, it will settle to the ground with a moderate thump. Some touchdowns were more moderate than others.

The majority of our time was spent scanning for other aircraft and, in low altitude hovers, we kept the pilot informed about how close the tail was to any obstacles. We sometimes got a bit too close for comfort.

To practice using the hoist, we used the forest penetrator attachment and tried to hit "bulls eye" on a target on the ground. Around five hundred feet out from the target, the pilot would lose sight of the target as it went under the aircraft. At that point the PJ would go on "hot mike" and talk the pilot in, giving "ahead," "left" or "right" adjustments. We couldn't lower the penetrator until after we were directly above the target to prevent uncontrollable oscillations in the cable. Oscillations were a problem and with the left hand we worked the cable in the opposite direction for some degree of control. We could call for minor corrections from a hover and the pilot wanted to be kept well informed on the height of the penetrator from the ground. We made a few jumps, but only during the day and on the land. We had simulated medical emergencies waiting on us, we then directed the helicopter back for recovery. Airsickness is not something that a veteran flier normally has a problem with. I lost my lunch only once when the pilots were practicing low altitude, high speed maneuvers. The cabin door and cargo ramp were both closed. The smell of JP-4 is bad enough when it's ventilated, it's nauseating when confined. Added to the heat in the cabin and changing G-forces of the twists and turns, I was feeling worse by the minute. My final mistake was looking out the window. We were only fifty feet off the ground doing one hundred sixty mph. The sight of the ground moving so quickly below made me loose it instantly. I had been carrying my airsick bag for ten minutes and almost held it back. The pilot had no problem opening the doors after that.

A note on the bulletin board at the chow hall caught my attention. Someone was driving to Oklahoma City for the Thanksgiving holiday and needed help with driving and expenses. My check ride was coming soon· and I was warned not to be late getting back and not to be getting into any trouble. We had five days that weren't going to be counted against our leave. If we didn't get back, we'd be AWOL.

It was too far for the amount of time we had. That is, we didn't get out of town in time to get back. We thought that if we held it under ninety mph that by 0800 we would be there. My ride couldn't afford to be late any more than I could. I slept as he took us out of Oklahoma and he woke me up just before we reached Colorado. The sun was already up and by afternoon I realized that I wouldn't make the briefing for the next day's flight. The eastern edge of the Rocky Mountains were well over the horizon and my foot rested a little heavier on the accelerator. This guy had a 1969 Chevy SS and it was comfortable. I was doing one of those stupid things you just don't do, doing a hundred thirty mph in a state you weren't born in or lived in. Still, it took over an hour to get close enough to the Rockies and for the traffic to get thick enough for me to idle it back a little bit. I was doing ninety when I saw the lights flashing in my rear view mirror.

The other guy was still asleep when I pulled the car over. We were both wearing our dress blues and as I stepped out I put on my beret. I watched as the officer slung open his door, launched himself from the drivers seat and put on his Smokey The Bear Hat. He glared square into my eyes, stepped forward and pointed a finger toward my face yelling, "I've been chasing you for forty-five miles. Get into my car!" I sat in the front seat with him as he took my license. I explained how important it was for me to be at Hill AFB. His reply was, "You're under arrest!"

"I need to wake up the owner of the car," I said as the officer was filling out his forms. "You don't own it? Yeah, get him up," he said.

"Hey, wake up man!" I yelled shaking him into consciousness. "This cop is putting me in jail and I can't talk him out of it." He grasped the magnitude of the situation immediately and ran directly back to the patrol car. The officer had stepped out and put his hand on his pistol. The guy held up his hands saying, "This man's a member of the United States Air Force's Pararescue team. He's just trained for a year and has his orders for Vietnam. He's leaving in a few days, but now you're going to put him in jail. My God, man. He's risking his life solely to save somebody else's life. Somebody he doesn't even know!"

The officer walked over to us, handed me my drivers license and said, "Get your ass in the passenger's seat and don't ever let me catch you driving in my state again."

"Yes sir," I assured him.

We arrived on base before 0700 and made the briefing, even having time for breakfast. "Somehow, McGuire," one of the instructors said, "I didn't think you'd make it back."

"You'll never know," I replied, "just how close it was."

An event occurred that brought the team back together again. It snowed hard enough to open the ski slopes. Carpenter invited me to go with him.

"Mike," I said, now that we were finally on a first name basis, "I don't know how to ski."

"It's easy," he said. "Just take the lift to the top of the mountain. By the time you get to the bottom, you'll know how to ski."

It seemed good enough for me. At the top of the mountain, the path turned sharply left. Also from the top, the only direction you have to go is down. Not knowing how to turn left, I went across the path and down the back side. Grabbing at a rock, I was able to stop and climb back up to Mike, with people I didn't even know laughing at me.

Mike taught me the snow plow, and explained that the skis turned on their edges. I rolled down the first half of the mountain, but after the slope flattened out a little and I had time to practice, I found myself getting the hang of it. The only thing that kept us off the slopes after that was our flight schedule.

I didn't really have orders for Vietnam. In fact, none of us did. Carpenter had orders for a base in Thailand, but they were canceled. Nixon had brought everyone out of Vietnam a few weeks after our graduation and a few days after the Colorado incident. My orders were for Fairchild AFB just outside of Spokane, Washington. I was going back to the survival school. Four guys were going to Clark AFB in the Philippines, and everyone else was being scattered.

We received our diplomas from Helicopter School, none of us really in a hurry to part company. For eleven months we had lived together so closely that we often thought and acted as one.

For it all to end so abruptly had not been considered and it was a bitter moment for all of us. Base transportation arrived early. I left alone with everything I owned in two duffel bags. It was early December. I was headed home for Christmas.

Chapter Nine

PCS Fairchild

Everything about my assignment to Fairchild was a screwup from the beginning. The airline lost my duffel bags, and it was two months before I got them back. By that time they had been around the world several times. It also took two months to get my pay straightened out, causing me to go to the Red Cross for an emergency loan.

During in-processing, I noted a gorgeous brunette. I thought that maybe this wouldn't be such a bad place after all, but before I could come up with a reason to get her name, she vanished. I would meet her later, but didn't realize it at the time and thought she was gone forever.

Fairchild seemed to be the favorite retirement location for PJs, so we were over staffed with tech and master sergeants. With Vietnam over, Fairchild absorbed several of the PJs returning from Asia.

I was assigned a trainer who refused the job. "Hell, I don't have any business training anybody. I'm retiring in six months. Get somebody else to do it."

He was a master sergeant and it really pissed him off when the senior master sergeant ordered him to be my trainer. He still didn't train me.

If the quarterly training requirements aren't met, you're removed from flight status and a lot of trouble is created. In those first two months I hadn't even been on one flight. They had less than thirty days to get me qualified on a new aircraft, complete my check ride, get at least twelve hours flying time and make two jumps. The senior master sergeant took over my training and completed all the necessary paper work only days before my flight pay would have stopped.

One reason everything was so slow was because two months before I arrived, a helicopter crashed and killed the entire crew including one PJ. The pilot was flying low over the Spokane River talking to the fishermen on the public address system. He never saw the high power lines crossing the river and flew straight into them, turning the helicopter upside down and falling into the water. The PJ had been well liked, and he was missed very much. I felt as if they were taking it out on me.

I not only had nothing to do, I had no one to do it with. I was the only occupant in the barracks. Everyone else lived off base. It was winter and the region was in a drought. It was the most depressing time I could remember. Things did get a little better, just before they got worse.

A PJ named Roger transferred in from Vietnam and moved into the barracks with me while we waited for our pay to catch up. We had nothing to do but watch TV and talk. "Hogan's Heroes" came on daily, and we spent time chatting while we watched. But Roger only spoke of Vietnam once. I thought he would tell me how he received a pronounced scar on his face, but instead he told me of how his best friend was killed.

Not knowing exactly where to start, he began with, "They gave me alot of medals, but they gave Dave alot more." I could see the gleam of a tear in his eye as he remembered back to Vietnam. He and Dave had trained together and were both sent straight to war. Both were very young.

"Four pilots were down at the same time. The two we picked up were several hundred yards apart and were both hurt. Dave and I were on different helicopters that day. Dave went down the penetrator on his team. I was the right gunner and hoist operator on mine.

"The pilots couldn't ride the penetrator, so I had to send the litter back down. After the pilot was on board, I sent the penetrator back down for the PJ."

Roger paused and swallowed hard. "We looked like sitting targets, floating just above the trees. But Charlie had alot of respect for rescue efforts. Not that he gave a damn about the humanitarian aspect of it, but that they knew that if they shot at us, fire was going to rain down on them from not only our mini-guns, but the Sandys providing close air support as well.

"But that day we spent too long in one spot. Charlie moved in and set up. Before we could complete our mission, Charlie opened up with everything he had. I could see muzzle flashes from small arms fire in the jungle below, and returned fire with the mini-gun. I poured thousands of rounds into the area. The Sandys came down then, strafing the jungle with machine gun fire and dropping napalm. We even had some F-4 Phantoms fly in from off-shore.

"We hovered there until both pilots and PJs were on board, then accelerated out of there as fast as we could. But it wasn't fast enough. I saw the missile trail as it left the ground and watched helplessly as it arced up, fishtailed twice, then flew right through the cargo ramp of Dave's Jolly Green. It hit the forward bulkhead inside and exploded in a ball of flame. The helicopter disintegrated and fell burning into the jungle."

Roger sat with an empty stare. Finally, he said "Let's don't talk about Vietnam anymore. It doesn't make me feel better at all."

Something did make Roger feel better, though. He had a distinct smile on his face one afternoon after I returned from a flight. He had met a WAF during lunch, and it was love at first sight. He was seeing her right after work.

Roger and I were going to share an apartment but events that were going to transpire that day would change our original plans. The girl he was dating already had an apartment and Roger informed me he was going to move in with her.

WE'RE ALL MAD, YOU KNOW

"She's sharing a room with another WAF," he informed me. "Come on out tonight and meet her."

When the apartment door opened, there stood the brunette from the in-processing briefing. A huge smile came over my face thinking that this was the roommate, and was available. My heart sank when Roger walked right up to her and planted one square on the mouth. Roger introduced us.

"Gary, this is Gloria. She's from Georgia, and quite proud to be a Georgia Peach."

It was obvious that no relationship would develop between Gloria and me, so I decided to leave. But Gloria stopped me.

"Why don't you move in with us, too? You can sleep on the couch, and by splitting the rent four ways, it would be easier on us all."

I might not have her affection, but a least I could have her company. And I couldn't help but think that, after all, if any man deserved her, it was Roger.

I moved in the next day.

I was placed on the flight schedule and assigned a new trainer.

For four months it was business as usual, flying support for the survival school. Every student was picked up with the hoist, and I became proficient after the first few hundred pickups. We were always careful in handling the cable. We ran it out its full length looking for frays regularly. Six of us ran it out inspecting it and we could have it replaced for so much as a fray. You can imagine our surprise when we learned that the cable had just broke on the flight that was out. The PJ reported that the student was sitting on the penetrator, his legs folded under him and three feet from the door in a twelve foot hover. The cable snapped just below his hand without any warning. It took a second and a half for the student to hit the ground breaking both of his legs. They immobilized him on a backboard and had him at the base hospital in five minutes. Just one of those things that happens.

We flew a lot of hours, and all in all it was getting mundane, but then came the First Annual Airway Heights Day Parade. They had asked if Pararescue could jump in, opening the ceremonies. During the briefing, we were told that a warm front was due in early afternoon and by jump time the winds might be too high, so plan to cancel. The jumpmaster asked us on the way to the airplane how badly we wanted to do this. We told him that if he'd go, then we'd go.

Over the drop zone, we could see the crowd watching as the first spotter 'chute was dropped. It landed fourteen counts north of the target.

"The winds are picking up," the pilot reported calmly. In fact they were already above the limit.

"Get ready McGuire," the jumpmaster ordered, "you're going on the next pass." He extended the count past the target to twenty, putting us out over a quarter of a mile beyond the target. He had guessed right, putting me and my team mate right on the target. The second team landed fifty yards down wind, but just after the last team jumped, we felt the first gust from the front. At least twenty mph and maybe thirty-five. At those speeds you lose your steering and go where the wind takes you. Devoe was on a collision course with a water tower. He crossed the target at three hundred feet, swinging back and fourth. He timed it just right for the parachute to pass over the tower as he swung past it and behind the tower on the other side, landing in a rocky field. We were a hit.

I only got to go to Mt. Calispell once, to play hide and seek with the students on the ground. With over one hundred GIs walking around in a ten mile radius you would think they would be easy to spot. Not so. When people look small, and dressed in green, it makes them disappear. We took three instructors up for a look around. The pilot asked me to have air sick bags ready for them because he intended to give them a ride they wouldn't forget. After only fifteen minutes of twisting, rolling and diving, all three heaved uncontrollably. When we set them down, they were ready to get off.

My troubles seemed to start soon after we returned to base.

My new trainer was an overzealous, born again PJ. He wasn't content with being at peace with God, he believed it was his duty to convert me. After saying no several times to going to church with him, he decided I was a hopeless sinner that refused to change his ways. He wasn't far from wrong. I had no intentions of confessing my sins and suffice it to say I partied pretty hard. I was getting to bed late and therefore, more often than not, I was late for work. We didn't work, but we were to at least show up on time. My trainer began writing me up.

WE'RE ALL MAD, YOU KNOW

I was called into Pappy LaCass's office one day. We called him Pappy because he was the oldest senior PJ in the Air Force, with thirty years service and eight stripes on his sleeve. He had every medal there was to receive except the Medal of Honor. It was said that he deserved that one too.

"Do you know why you're here?" Pappy asked me.

"No," I answered honestly, "I don't."

He took five pieces of paper out of his desk and handed them to me. They were letters of reprimand.

I looked on the bottom of each where my signature belonged and on each was written, "Airman refuses to sign." I didn't bother reading the reprimand and threw them back on his desk. "This is the first I've ever seen these," I assured him.

"OK," he said, "look at this." He handed me my airman's performance report, a yearly evaluation that everyone receives. The report grades you in nine areas. Each area is graded 0 through 9. Zero applies if you are dead. Nine means you're God-like. PJs normally get 9's right down the line. I had two 0s, two 1s, three 2s, and two 3s. I looked up at Pappy with complete astonishment.

"People in Leavenworth get better APRs than this!" he said abruptly. "I haven't been here very long and I don't really know you, but I do know that to be a PJ you have to have something on the ball. I just received your new orders for Okinawa. I'm going to wait before sending this report forward. Stay out of trouble for the next six weeks."

Apparently he was asking too much because my next stunt was one of those stupid things you just don't do. The standardization team was coming to Fairchild and they were scheduled to be on my flight for my yearly check

168

ride. The thought of the standardization team sent chills down the back of the best. They went around the world making sure everyone did the same thing the same way. They had the authority to ground you on the spot.

I studied my manuals again, but the night before the flight was one of those nights when just about everybody I knew came by the house. At 0200 the party was still on, so I had to leave in order to get any sleep. I kept my barracks room inspection ready for just such emergencies. I set the alarm for 0600. The briefing was scheduled for 0700 and the flight was to take off at 0800.

"McGuire!!"

I sprang straight up in bed. The alarm was ringing. The clock said 0805. Pappy LaCasse was standing over me. "Get dressed and come to my office."

I couldn't believe it. I missed my check ride. They were in the air and my shit was about to hit the fan. I was dressed and in Pappy's office in some kind of quick.

We sat there looking at each other. There was nothing I could say in my defense. Pappy finally broke the silence. "I wouldn't believe anyone who told me the story of what I just saw. The only reason anyone is going to believe me is because I am Pappy LaCasse. Right now, I'm the only thing standing between you and a court martial."

He sat back and looked up, then back at me. "I saw your car parked in front of the barracks and waited till straight up 0800 before going inside. Gary, I heard the alarm from downstairs. Each step I took up was about as loud as I could stomp. I stood at the door and all I heard was the alarm ringing. When I tried the knob, the door

169

opened and there you lay. I stepped inside your room and watched you for two or three minutes. You were sound asleep." He paused again. I still hadn't said a word.

"The facts that might save your ass are one, you were on base. Two, you made at least an effort by setting the alarm and three, I am your witness. I'm going to reschedule your check ride. I expect you to perform flawlessly. We'll discuss what happens to you next, depending on you."

Pappy had taken over the case and the standardization team left without even talking to me. Pararescue is the only career field in the military that does not answer to officers. The senior PJ sergeant is in charge of PJs and Pappy was as senior as you can get. Pappy suggested that I move back on base. Even with all the trouble I created for him, he still showed me the courtesy of making an order not sound like an order. I moved back.

Pappy and two other sergeants rode with me on my renewed check ride asking every question they could think of. I had to remove the seats and attach the stretcher system, work the hoist, put the penetrator on bulls eye from one hundred feet, then jump into a simulated wreck scene to treat and evacuate the injured. My patient's injuries were devised by the same sergeant who wrote my less than sterling performance report. When he finished detailing the injuries I was to treat, they were so extensive my patient was considered FUBAR'ed (Fouled Up Beyond All Recognition). When I couldn't remember the term paradoxical respirations, he declared that I had killed my patient. Pappy wasn't fooled. In all, he was satisfied with my performance.

WE'RE ALL MAD, YOU KNOW

The following day, back in Pappy's office, the atmosphere was more relaxed, yet somber. "The squadron commander wants to see you. Without his signature we can't release your orders. Even then, with this bad APR I'm required to hold you here for six months evaluation. At that point, you either work out or you'll be dishonorably discharged. Come back and see me when the colonel's through with you."

The colonel just wanted to talk about those five unsigned reports. Any one that refuses to sign a report is required to tell the squadron commander why. He believed me when I told him I hadn't seen them and then we talked about what it meant to be a PJ. I told him it was a drastic change from training so hard, then not getting to do what I was trained for.

He shook my hand and he wished me good luck. It took me by complete surprise and I stepped back at attention and saluted sharply. He returned my salute and I dropped my hand back to attention, did an about face and marched from his office.

Pappy and the squadron's first sergeant, a non-PJ, were waiting for me when I returned. A large stack of copies of my orders were on his desk.

"Officially," Pappy began, "you're on administrative hold. Unofficially," he continued, "there are still thirty days before your orders take effect. It'll take me at least that long to forward this paper work. You have more than thirty days leave coming. If you and your orders were to 'disappear', and thirty days from now you just showed up in Okinawa, I doubt if they would send you back."

171

Pappy and the first sergeant stood up and left the room, not saying another word. I sat there a moment looking at the stack of orders. A rush went through me as I realized what just happened. Pappy was letting me go.

"Thank you Pappy, thank you Pappy, thank you Pappy," I kept saying to myself as I jumped up and grabbed my orders.

The hall was clear, and although I didn't see anyone as I got into my car and left, I was sure every PJ in the place was watching me. I made one stop at my locker, one stop at my barracks room, then drove straight off base before anyone could change their mind. From off base I called the administrative office, telling them to place me on leave and permanent change of station.

"You can't do that," the voice said. "You've got to come in here and sign the proper forms."

"Do whatever you have to do," I said back. "I'm already gone." I made a few stops in Spokane to say good-bye and drove east.

I learned a lesson in life during my drive to Oklahoma. If you see a line of cars ahead of you in the distance and nobody's passing the lead car, the lead car will be a cop. I learned too late, (that is one of those stupid things you just don't do) as I was doing ninety mph when I caught up with them. The road made a left bend and a small town was just ahead. The officer pulled left into a gas station. Across the road was a hitchhiker. I pulled up to him and he opened the car door. "You really don't want to ride with me," I said as he sat down. "I was speeding across the desert and the cops are fixin' to bust me." The officer was just pulling in behind me. He ordered the hitchhiker away from the car and looked at my drivers licenses.

"You realize you're in Utah don't you?" he asked. "You have a Washington tag and an Oklahoma driver's license. Where are your drugs?"

"Drugs?" I questioned, "I don't have any drugs."

He searched for ten minutes but came up with nothing. I didn't have the registration to the car either.

"How do I know this car isn't stolen?" he asked in anger.

"I'll call the sergeant I bought it from and he can verify my story," I reasoned.

"Call him," he ordered.

There was no one home and I wasn't about to call the PJ section.

"I'll keep trying this number," the officer said. "If I find out you've lied to me, I'll be pissed. I know you were speeding but I didn't get you on radar. Just remember, you can't outrun my radio." He gave me back my licenses, the hitchhiker jumped in, and we were off.

Fifteen minutes later we were still laughing when I saw the lights in my mirror. I pulled off the road and waited for him.

He came out yelling, "I told you, you shouldn't lie to me. I got hold of that sergeant and he reported this car stolen three days ago!"

"What!" I said, "that's not funny. Why would he say such a thing? Let's go call him back and find out why he said that."

The officer went back through the car again turning to me saying, "I know you have drugs in there, I just can't

173

find them. I didn't get a hold of that sergeant, I just wanted to see if you could tell the same story twice. I did get you on radar at seventy-five but hell, I won't write a ticket for five miles over the speed limit. Go on, get out of my state."

I was running out of states to get out of. I was pulled over and searched in every state between there and home, but never got a ticket.

Chapter Ten

PCS Kadena

The month passed by quickly once I was with my family. They had moved to a rural address near Chandler, Oklahoma. I had to call Mom and Dad for directions to their new home. You wonder if you're unwanted when your parents move and you don't know where. Of course, they welcomed me home. It seemed like only the next day when they dropped me off at Will Rogers World Airport for my trip half way around the world. Mom was worried, thinking she may never see me again.

"Can't you quit now and do something a little less dangerous?" she pleaded.

I kissed her on the cheek and stepped inside the gang plank that lead to the airplane. I was twenty-one and hoped I had finally grown up.

There was a short layover in San Francisco to wait for the connecting flight. From a distance the man in jump boots with bloused blues and maroon beret stood out prominently. I must have been just as obvious as he noticed me at about the same time. I was wearing two stripes and he was wearing four, a staff sergeant.

He was stationed in Okinawa and had been in the States on leave, his first time back in over three years. When I told him I was coming out of Fairchild he said, "So, how's Pappy?"

"You know Pappy Lacasse?" I asked surprised.

"Every PJ knows Pappy," he said matter-of-factly. "How did you like working for him?"

"I think he is the fairest, most sincere man I've ever met in my life."

"That's Pappy," he noted.

The flight took us to Anchorage, Alaska, with a two hour lay over. It's hard to believe that it's shorter than going straight across, but it is. Still, it's a long way, taking ten or so hours at nearly the speed of sound. The PJ didn't want to talk about what I might expect. He just didn't talk much.

The wind blew hot and had a distinctive tropical smell. I stepped off the airplane and into my new life at Kadena Air Base, Okinawa. We stood outside waiting for our bags to clear customs. The PJ said I could spend the night in the alert shack and took me there after we collected our bags. It had living quarters that were rarely used, and I could stay there until I found a permanent place. He and PJ Randy McComb came back soon to get me.

"Nate wants to meet you," they told me. "We'll take you to his house." It was nearly dark and still hot.

Nate was Master Sergeant Nathaniel Smith, our NCOIC (Non-Commissioned-Officer-In-Charge). He lived on base with his wife and two girls. He was a large man with eyes that looked square at you and a face that spoke authority. His smile and charm made him a hero's hero.

"Have you got a copy of your orders with you?" he asked me after the introductions and 'how was your flight?'

"No, but I'll bring you a copy tomorrow," I said, trying to be helpful.

"Do that," he said. "Usually I know when someone's coming," he continued. "Last I heard about you, was that your orders were canceled. How did you manage to get here?"

"No one told me they were canceled," I replied in confusion.

Nate broke out in hearty laughter and the others were shaking their heads and laughing too. I failed to see the humor.

"Don't take this wrong," Nate said still laughing. "You're not at all what I would have imagined. Why don't you stay tonight in the alert shack and I'll send someone to get you in the morning."

On the way back, I wondered not only about what they had heard about me, but how many PJs around the world had heard it.

As promised, the next morning some more PJs came by to pick me up. Our section was just across the street from the flight line, and one block from base operations. It was a two story building. The officers occupied the upstairs, the entire PJ troop downstairs, with the flight mechanics and ground crew in an attached building. We had a separate parachute packing room and an out building that housed the SCUBA gear and our boat. During my walk around I learned that Kadena had the largest and most active PJ section in the world. There were twenty-two of us. It seemed like a lot but two were always on alert on the C-130, one on the HH-53 and one on the HH-3E (we didn't have any Hueys). Two or more PJs were always TDY (temporary duty) on another 130. Of the other two C-130s, one was flying locally with two PJs and one was always being fixed. We had three HH-53s and two HH-3Es. Scheduling was a nightmare. Just as a matter-of-fact, Nate was one of only three black men in all of Pararescue. He was so human, that the thought of color simply never came up. He was as respected as Pappy and they were in fact, good friends.

Nate was expecting me. "You've got the rest of today and tomorrow to get settled into the barracks and processed into the base. I talked to Pappy this morning. He was glad to hear you made it. He's sending me your records. I have you scheduled for a check ride on the C-130 in two days. You'll be going to Clark in the Philippines next week for the Apollo Capsule recovery training. When you get back we'll check you out on the 53. I understand that you're not qualified on the 3-E."

"That's right sergeant, I'm not."

"Call me Nate. It might be sometime before we get around to qualifying you on it but sooner or later we will.

WE'RE ALL MAD, YOU KNOW

You don't mind spending the bulk of your flight time on a C-130 do you?"

"Mind? That would be fine with me."

Nate eased back looking at me through narrowed eye, "You owe Pappy LaCasse more than you will ever know," he concluded. "Don't let him down."

"If it's more than I know Nate, then it's one hell of a lot. I'll go get processed in now."

"You're dismissed," he said with a proud look on his face. Nate had that quality of making you want to do things for him. He never had to give an order. Everything he said was taken as an order.

I was really disappointed with my barracks. PJs, mechanics and load masters for the whole ARRS Squadron were stacked two to a room. We had no air conditioning either.

"It's not as bad as it could be," one on the PJs noted. "At least we're TDY from here some of the time."

Processing in was a little difficult because of the way I had left Fairchild. Nate was not the only one that wasn't expecting me. It seemed the entire Air Force wondered what I was doing there. But there I was so they did what they had to. Seems everyone I met that day had a comment like, "You PJs never play by the rules," or, "Only a PJ could get away with this."

I got back to the section in time to study the C-130 operations manual. It had been a year since I last thought of this stuff, but a refresher brought it all back. The check ride went without a hitch.

To fly from Okinawa to the Philippines on a C-130 took four hours. We spent four more hours flying around in

179

circles doing touch and goes. By the time we got off the airplane the PJ section was closed. Everyone else got temporary quarters, but I told the pilot I knew some of the guys in the barracks and that I would stay there.

"Hey!" I yelled from outside, "Any PJs living up there?"

Setchfield was the first to look out his window.

"McGuire!" he yelled back. "What the hell are you doing here? Come on up."

We had a great reunion. McLafferty and Geza were there too and within minutes we were off base to show me around the town. We drank a lot of beer and told a lot of stories.

"You just squeezed in under the wire again," Setchfield told me. "This is going to be the last Apollo class ever taught. The last Apollo shot is going up in two weeks. After that, it's all obsolete."

We were going to make three SCUBA jumps, the last one being at night. A Navy Seal team from Subic Bay would tow the capsule out about five miles into the South China Sea with our objective being to land down drift from the capsule and let it come to us. Even in a calm sea the capsule moves about two to three mph. Add a little wind and it speeds up quick. You can't out-swim it. As it comes crashing toward you, you line yourself up directly in its path and try to time it so that at the top of a wave you and the capsule collide. The PJ had to tread water like crazy to get as high out of the water as possible to grab a special sea anchor hooking ring designed to be on the leading edge of the drifting craft. In preparation, one side of the reserve parachute pack was already released from the harness. The

180

WE'RE ALL MAD, YOU KNOW

PJ who had hold of the ring in the left hand would ride the capsule like a bucking bronco as he unsnapped the remaining side of the reserve and hooked the parachute to the ring. This done, he would simply grab the rip cord handle and let go. As the reserve deployed, it would catch water and bring the capsule to a stop.

"For Gods sake you guys," the instructor pleaded, "don't drop your reserve into the ocean." That would be another one of those stupid things you just don't do.

The C-130 would then drop a line of containers holding the flotation device, rafts and other equipment. It was a job for three men to install the flotation device, but it could be done. In practice all six of us in the class worked together. This was my first SCUBA jump in over a year. They told me I cleared the door with room to spare.

The trip back to port took several hours, but we had plenty of room to move around as there were only a dozen people on the landing craft. Near shore, we passed a landing craft the same size as ours but it was full of Marines. They were side to side and back to front packed in like sardines. We agreed that ours was the way to live. We transferred our gear to trucks and again to the airplane for the flight back to Clark. It was well after dark before the salt water residues were washed off and all of our gear hung to dry, including the parachutes. We had a lot of sixteen hour days.

The night jump was a disaster from the word go. We were told to be at the briefing at 1000 hours. We didn't arrive until 1030. I could have been on time, but it was more important to stand with my team and be late. The pilot was annoyed. The PJ NCOIC just shook his head.

WE'RE ALL MAD, YOU KNOW

There were six of us, and I was the junior. I didn't feel so guilty this time. Briefings are where the pilot gives the details about what was going to happen on the flight. We caught the last words he had to say which were, ."..have your gear on the airplane by 1100. I want to get out of here early."

None of us had prepared any of our gear, and at 1100 we were just loading the truck. We were stowing our gear on board at 1115. The pilot walked by with disgust on his face. "Don't hassle the man that works in the back if all you do is drive the bus," one of the PJs said, adding a respectful "sir" at the end.

"Watch it," was the pilots reply.

We were dropped off at Subic Bay while the airplane took off and practiced flying. We all played with the pinball machines while we waited for the sun to go down. The 130 returned around 2030, but still we had to fly around for over an hour before it got dark.

Our target was a rotating beacon with four stationary lights around it. From the door, we could see a thousand lights from small fishing boats. "I don't see a rotating beacon," the jumpmaster reported to the pilot.

"Stand by," he said. A few moments later he came back. "They're reporting trouble with the light," he explained. "It won't rotate."

"I can't tell one light from another," the PJ replied. "They need to move the target out further."

Another two hours of flying around, which kept us geared up for three hours, and now I needed to pee. But the pilot had refused us permission to get undressed. He was punishing us for our insubordination.

182

WE'RE ALL MAD, YOU KNOW

The target was about ten miles out now and free of all the clutter. Inside the aircraft the red lights were turned on except for one white light at the forward bulkhead. The jumpmaster asked that it be turned off, but the pilot was still pissed and answered, "Just don't look forward."

The lesson here was obvious. Don't piss off the bus driver.

We were all so miserable by now that all we wanted was out of the airplane. I drew the first team and I was ready to jump. We were on final approach and I was feeling strong. The jumpmaster slapped the platform yelling, " Stand in the door!"

I had been standing with my head cocked to one side to avoid the white light. As my head turned to focus on the door my vision crossed the white light. That's right, it's one of those stupid things you just don't do because I was instantly blinded. I couldn't make out the edges of the door. Everything was black. I groped with my hands as my vision began to show outlines. I managed to get set just as the jumpmaster slapped me on the thigh. I hesitated. It just didn't feel right. I reset myself and jumped with all my might into the windy darkness.

I looked up at the ghostly image of my parachute being blown past me by the prop wash. I already had twists in my suspension lines from the risers, just over my head to nearly the skirt of the canopy. It was the dreaded cigarette roll, and I was building speed fast. I grabbed the risers, pulling them apart and bicycling my legs. I stopped spinning and the twists began to unwind.

"This is taking entirely too long," I said to myself, deciding to deploy my reserve. I tried to hold the pack closed as I pulled the rip cord handle in order to grab some parachute and throw it out and away from me. It didn't work. The spring loaded pilot 'chute got away from me, catching air as I fell out from under it. A giant white cloud of parachute whizzed by only inches from my face, but instead of billowing out and stopping my fall, it wrapped around my main 'chute from the spin of the untwisting suspension lines.

I looked out into the void. "Next time," I told myself, "I gotta remember to eject my main before I deploy the reserve."

An overwhelming sensation of calm came over me as I realized I was about to die. A warm wave flowed through my body. It seemed like it was taking an awful long time, and I wondered what it was going to be like.

The rags I had dangling over my head did at least keep me falling feet first and slowed me down to not much more than one hundred mph. I thought to raise my hands straight over my head and tilt my fins up, slicing into the water.

For a brief moment I seriously wondered if I was dead. No, I decided. Dead people don't think and I was even moving my arms and legs.

Most of me was wrapped in suspension lines as I rose back up through them. The two parachutes landed just beside me. The sight of the silk sinking, floating and drifting all at once and the feel and taste of the salt water and the vastness of the ocean around me made me shiver. I wondered about the depth. There was probably five miles of water below me. Yes sir, we were really having fun now.

WE'RE ALL MAD, YOU KNOW

I put my mask on and my regulator in my mouth and settled under the water, trying to untie myself. I was getting nowhere fast.

When I came back up I heard Geza calling my name. It took him and the SEAL in their motorized raft ten minutes to find me. My flare had been ripped off on impact, so calling back and fourth was all we had left. The strobe light attached to my shoulder was still attached but it had quit working. That made me wonder if I didn't hit harder than I thought.

"Get in here and get me out of this," I demanded, once I had been found.

"Relax," Geza said, "you still have ten minutes before that sinking chute starts dragging you down."

"That's comforting. Now get your ass in here and start cutting this son-of-a-bitch off of me!"

After getting it off we decided to let it sink, not that we could have gotten it back if we had wanted to. As we neared the real jump zone, we found the jumpmaster.

"Don't worry about me, go find Farly. He's had a malfunction. And watch out for my para..."

Too late, it just wrapped up in the propeller. We could hear Farley, he was in near panic. "Come on Geza," I said as I dove out of the raft. "It's only a quarter of a mile."

During the swim, the thoughts of sharks entered my mind. They feed at night and they like things that splash on the surface. I reminded myself that these thoughts are normal. It's how you act on these thoughts that count.

Farly wasn't handling it very well. We kept him calm enough, though he was sure the parachute was dragging him down as we spoke. We finally got him cut free. In

Farley's defense, he was tied up pretty tight and his 'chute had completely sunk. At long last, we were all aboard the landing craft, minus some of our equipment.

Farley and I had the same malfunction. The jumpmaster assured me that I had cleared the door and Farly felt sure he had cleared it as well. We compared logs from our back pack and both 'chutes had been packed by the same rigger. Had this been a land jump, we would both have been dead. I decided at this point that I would never jump with a 'chute I hadn't packed myself.

"Who doesn't feel proficient in installing the floatation device? Well good," the instructor said, not giving anybody time to answer, "then we can consider this exercise concluded before we kill somebody."

It was early in the morning when we returned to Clark. The sun was well up before we got to bed.

Upon returning to Okinawa, I found my name on both the flight schedule and the proficiency schedule and would be taking my turn on alert. They obviously didn't intend to send me back to Fairchild. Then Nate walked in.

"McGuire," he said loudly with a smile, "we heard you nearly went to Davy Jones' Locker. What have you got to do today?"

"It wasn't that close," I said modestly, "and I'm not scheduled for anything until the night land jump day after tomorrow."

"Good," he replied. "Stay close, you're going with me to White Beach."

I still felt very new. I had been stationed here for fourteen days and this was only the fifth time I had been in this building. Of the twenty-two PJs stationed here, only five, including Nate and myself were there at that time. There were two offices against one wall. The rest of the area was large and open. A living room arrangement and coffee pot were in the middle of the room. I made myself comfortable. Nate wasn't long and stepped quickly in long strides. "Keep up with me McGuire," he said walking towards the door. I jumped up and matched his stride.

Stepping outside, we both put on our berets at the same time, molding the extra material to the right. Every PJ seemed to wear their beret a little different. This was the first time that I really felt that I belonged to the finest, most professional, elite team of men in the United States Air Force, and maybe the world.

"I'm going to back the truck up to the boat," Nate stated. "Guide me back, will ya?"

"Sure," I replied and broke into double time to wait for him by the trailer. Using aircraft hand signals I backed him in, right on the spot. It was a thirty minute drive getting the rig through the narrow, crowded roads to the naval station at White Beach on the south end of the island, not far from the infamous "Suicide Cliffs" of WWII.

Nate went inside the operations room while I waited outside. "The airplane's just now taking off," he said as he came out. "They'll be on station in ten minutes."

"I'd like to back the boat into the water," I said to Nate as he was opening the door.

"We don't have time for any backing lessons right now Gary."

"That's OK," I said. "They didn't have time for me at Fairchild either."

He didn't deserve that, but the look on his face said it was OK. "You have one chance. The first time you have to stop you step out. Is that clear?"

"That's clear," I said and slid behind the wheel.

Nate couldn't know that during my sport SCUBA days that I had backed a lot of boats. He was amazed that I backed as straight as an arrow. I simply explained that I had done it once or twice.

The boat was nice. It had an inboard diesel engine and power lift-out drive. It moved at thirty mph and had enough room for eight men and their equipment. We picked up six PJs that afternoon, some of them I met for the first time. They were all treating me like some kind of hero for having survived a parachute double malfunction.

"Do you think you can drive this thing back?" Nate asked me after we got the boat out of the water.

"If you'll point me in the right direction," I replied.

The day came when the last Apollo mission was to splash down. Everything we had was in the air. The odds against them missing the splash-down area and landing in the particular region I was responsible for were not astronomical. It did happen once, on the Apollo 8 mission, and it could happen again. But it didn't. They landed right on target and the Navy Seals were waiting.

That didn't mean that we ran out of things to do. It was six months before the pattern of our routine became clear. Since everyone was told on a need-to-know policy, it wasn't often that PJs knew why the aircraft was going where it was going. Though usually we were escorting some kind of aircraft across the ocean, it could have been the President for all I knew. It was happening so often, that we had to rush training requirements at the end of each quarter.

Some mornings, as many as twelve PJs would show up at the section. If you were on alert, you briefed at 0700, "cocked" the aircraft at 0800, meaning having it ready to go at a moments notice, and kind of hung around by the radio for the next twenty-four hours. If you were scheduled for a flight, you showed up for that flight's briefing time, and flew away. If you were crew resting, you crew rested. Each man spent one week at the Army hospital emergency room at Naha, in an ever changing rotation. If you were jumping, you got your gear ready and jumped. Two and sometimes three PJs were out for three day walks in the jungle on the northern tip of Okinawa, and one PJ manned a remote station in Taiwan.

If you had nothing to do, you showed up before 0800. "Everyone else has to be at work on time," Nate said. "We're no different."

Actually, we were very different. Everyone else was standing at attention somewhere with some lieutenant walking around them writing up demerits. We were drinking coffee in the living room. Everyone else went to their jobs. We went to the gym. Nate kept the key to the base gym and we checked it out from him. We got very good at racket ball. We would leave the gym around 1045, go to the barracks for a shower, and be back at the section by 1145. At noon we went to chow, then back to work by 1300. I worked in the SCUBA section. We'd empty the drying racks, refill scuba tanks, keep everything, including the boat, clean and operational ready. It took a couple of hours.

I had been there only a couple of months when Nate called me into his office. "Gary," he looked at me very seriously, "the sergeant in charge of the SCUBA section got his orders. I'm looking for someone to take his place. You've only got two stripes but I'm considering putting you in charge over there." He leaned forward looking at me even harder in the eye than usual. "Do you think you can handle the job?"

"I can handle it, Nate."

"The job's not yours yet," he said as if he wasn't so sure. "I want you to prepare a class on diving and present it to the entire section. You have two weeks. Dismissed."

My old sport SCUBA days were really paying off. From memory I was able to put together an entire lesson plan complete with demonstrations on the chalk board and a forty question test at the end.

The class was quite an event. It took the squadron commander's help to make sure that nothing else was scheduled for that day. I had twenty-one seasoned PJs grading me on how well I taught them. They scored well on the test after listening to my lecture for nearly two hours. When the test was over, they all shook my hand and the job was mine. It was only one of several times I said to myself, "thank you Pappy." I still wonder how he kept me from losing any stripes but I still had both of them and now was the most junior PJ ever put in charge of anything, in spite of my poor APR. A couple of other PJs wanted the job, because it meant you got to "pilot the boat." But Nate gave it to me.

WE'RE ALL MAD, YOU KNOW

Ah, that infamous APR of mine. Randy Mccomb, a well-respected PJ told me, "Now that I know you better, I know you've been torpedoed. But every PJ in the world knows the name Gary McGuire, the worst PJ in history."

Some distinction, but these people were certainly my friends and I was happier there than at any other time I could remember. When I told him about the standardization team check ride that I had slept through, he just said, "I already know."

At 1600 hours the doors were all locked, and out of a five gallon Igloo cooler we all drank Harvey Wallbangers. This, I thought, was surely something else that only a PJ could get away with.

"Nate wants to see you, McGuire," was the message. When I reported to him he said, "I'd like your opinion on your living quarters."

"It's a WWII GI barrack," I answered. "And hot."

"Let's go for a ride. There's something I want you to see."

He drove only a mile to some one-level, cement block barracks. "These were pilot living quarters until yesterday," Nate explained. "I'm trying to arrange for Pararescue to occupy it, but only if you guys want it."

It was air conditioned, we would each have our own room, and it was across the street from the chow hall.

"Who wouldn't be happy living here?" I asked.

We moved in that night.

As airman in charge of the SCUBA section, I answered to Master Sergeant Vic Madoma. He was from the Philippines and married to a local woman. Many of the sergeants were married to oriental women and some had not been back in the States for as many as seven years. I don't remember the occasion but the wives cooked a dinner for us at Vic's house one night. The food was delicious and the sake was hot. Vic and Nate told some hilarious stories, at least we were drunk enough so that they seemed that funny. Vic couldn't finish his last toast as he fell forward, face first into a bowl of rice. I woke up in Vic's front yard. PJs were laid out all over the house.

We were TDY often. Three times a month per PJ. The flights normally went to Osan, Korea, for an overnight stay. From there to the Philippines for another over-nighter before returning to Okinawa. One incident in Korea nearly ended it for me and my partner.

The pilot told us to be at the airplane by 0900 for a 1000 take off. We made a bee line off base and partied all night.

The next morning I looked at the girl I woke up with and screamed, "Oh my God!" I looked at the clock and screamed, "Oh my God!" It was 0910. I had done it again. Pappy is going to kill me, I thought to myself.

I banged on my partners door. "Get up!" I yelled, "I'll call a taxi." It was 0955 when we got on base. I kept watching the sky toward the end of the flight line expecting to see our 130 climbing at any moment. When the taxi pulled up at base Ops, we saw the airplane getting ready in the take off position. It was 1005. We grabbed our baggage and ran full tilt across the flight line, taxi ways and into the field. I heard the sirens coming up behind us. The sky cops were closing fast across the field. Lights were flashing and the siren was getting louder. They caught up with us just as we reached the runway. The loadmaster lowered the steps at the crew entrance as the sky cops were jumping out of their truck. We never broke stride, running within a foot of the propellers and into the aircraft. The pilot let off the brake before the door was even shut, leaving the sky cops to wonder what they should do next. We hooked up to the intercom reporting, "PJs on board, sir."

"Glad you guys could make it," the pilot reported back as we left the ground. "We made up some malfunctions to buy you guys some time."

"Thank you very much," was all I could think of to say.

The loadmaster told us that was the slowest any airplane had ever taxied to a runway. We knew that this was one of those things only a PJ could get away with. It was also one of those stupid things you just don't do.

The flight to the Philippines took five hours, but PJs seldom landed with the airplane. The first pass took us over the drop zone and a spotter 'chute was dropped to check the count. On the third pass we were out of the airplane. Setchfield and McLafferty were usually on the ground waiting.

"We've got a new NCOIC," Ed informed me during one of my TDYs to Clark.

"Colvert?"

"No, but you're close. It's Kee."

It was a pleasure seeing him again as we exchanged polite hellos' and he congradulated me for making the team. It didn't really surprise him. By the time we left Lackland, we were expecting to make it.

Another party and another flight home.

193

WE'RE ALL MAD, YOU KNOW

* * *

Sometimes we would go to Guam, Hong Kong, Thailand or Japan. But the most sought after TDY ever was coming up and everybody wanted in on it. There would be a one day layover on Midway Island, two days in Hawaii and two days in Alaska. The fight was on for one of the two seats. Some pulled rank, others called in favors. The names on the schedule board changed several times.

A week before the flight, I pulled a Saturday alert. My team mate came to me saying Nate had asked him if we would tile the floor in the living room along with the rest of the open bay. He said it wasn't an order but if Nate wanted it, Nate got it. It took us all day. We even found some white tiles and laid a large PJ in the middle. When we finished, the other PJ, a highly decorated true hero, patted me on the back for the fine job I had helped him do. "If there's ever anything I can do for you," he said, "just ask."

"There is one thing," I said. "I would like to be on that flight to Hawaii."

He looked at me as if to say that was a little bit too much to ask but said seriously, "I'll see what I can do."

Monday afternoon everybody wanted to know what my name was doing on the schedule board for the flight. It was also the last change made. It proved to be the most eventful flight of my life.

The pilot was a lieutenant colonel, second in command of the entire 33rd. ARRS Squadron. A major was co-pilot, and every other position was filled with the most senior for that post.

194

WE'RE ALL MAD, YOU KNOW

I stepped on the airplane with my two stripes. My team mate was my floor laying buddy. Our mission was to escort a two engine, WWII airplane as far as Alaska. The ARRS there would escort her the rest of the way to the States. She was headed for a museum, if she made it.

It's far enough across the Pacific as it is. This museum piece was so slow, we had to perform 'S' turns back and forth across her flight path in order to keep up with her. We had to buckle up in our bunks or risk falling on the floor when we slept. Midway was a long time coming.

I sleep well in airplanes. I could even sleep while waiting to jump. On the ground in Midway, I was well rested. Goonie birds were everywhere. I did all the simple things people do: ate chow, watched an early movie with the thirty or so men stationed there, and walked completely around the island. I tried to imagine the fierce battle that raged there not that many years ago.

It took longer than I thought and I got to my room near the flight line about midnight. Some of the crew were playing poker a few doors down so I sat in for about an hour. I had just laid down and thought about the loud music coming from outside when the music suddenly stopped and a voice cried, "Somebody come down here and look at this!"

I was out of my bed and outside that quick. Three people I had never seen before were looking up at the sky. A bright white light, about the size of the noon-day sun, was several hundred feet directly above us and obviously climbing. As its distance increased the light grew steadily less in intensity and it maintained a steady course straight up. There wasn't a cloud in the sky, and it was a moonless

195

night. We watched in silence as this light became the brightest star in the sky. After a minute or so, one of the guys broke the silence.

"It looks just like any other star now," he said. A moment or two later another said, "It's still fading."

It became no brighter than the dimmest star. "See that?" one of them shouted, "It's moved right, now left."

"Anybody see it any more?"

"No," we replied. I dropped my head down for the first time after what seemed like several minutes.

"What did you guys see before I got out here?" I asked.

One of them began "We were standing here, and from out of nowhere this incredibly bright light appeared over the water past the end of the runway. It started moving forward and that's when I turned off the radio and yelled for someone to come out. It moved really fast and stopped right over the runway, then shot straight up. That's when you got here."

I noted that it didn't make any noise or generate any wind. They agreed. We all looked back up as if there was something to see, then back down again.

"I'm sorry," I said. "I can't tell anybody that I saw this. It could bring ridicule to my unit and I can't risk that."

"Yeah," one other agreed. "Everyone would think we were nuts." I went back inside and laid in my bunk.

"Why me Lord?" I asked. "Why did you have me see a sight such as this?"

The following morning, the crew was assembled around the airplane and the colonel stepped up near me. We nodded to each other and I felt I should say something so I recounted a dream to him I once had. "I could feel all the sensations of flight," I explained. "I could even see the ground as if looking from a height." He said he too has had such a dream and it was not uncommon to people that fly a lot.

Not too long after take off, the co-pilot went to his bunk leaving the seat open. "McGuire, are you on the head set?" the Colonel asked.

"Yes sir," I replied.

"Come on up and take the co-pilots seat." I think everybody on board was as surprised as I was. I carefully climbed past the navigator and flight engineer settling into the right seat and hooking into the intercom. "Buckle up," was his first order. I did. "All you need to know," he began, "is your horizon level and this little floating ball. If the ball moves right, step on the right rudder. If it moves left, step on the left rudder. If you're nosing down, pull back on the stick. If you're nose is up, push it forward a little. Remember, step on the ball. When you're ready, hold the stick."

The stick had two handles that fit well within your hands. Buttons, knobs and triggers were all over it.

"I'm ready," I said softly. The colonel flipped one switch on the panel turning off the automatic pilot. For a few moments the airplane stayed on course. I could see the propellers spinning in my periphery and felt the sheer size of the C-130 through the controls in my hands. The horizon indicator showed that we were beginning to nose down a little. I put some pressure against the stick. Still we kept nosing down so I pulled a little harder. It wouldn't come up.

"Heavy isn't it?" the colonel noted. "There's a trim button by your finger. Press that and it'll make it a little easier."

I pressed the button and the stick fell in my lap. The plane climbed hard, pulling several 'G's.

Shit! I thought, and pushed the stick forward. We went into a steep dive. *Damn!* I thought, and eased it back but still I over-corrected. As I was see-sawing the bubble drifted right, but I stepped on the left peddle thinking to bring the ball back but that only made it worse.

We were flying nearly sideways when the pilot took the controls saying, "I have the airplane," and straightened us back out. "It's OK," he said. "Everyone has a little trouble at first. Go ahead and try again." After ten minutes I nearly had us in straight and level flight.

"I have the airplane," the colonel stated as he put his hands on the controls. "Good job."

Who did he think he was kidding? I was sweating, and the people in the back, who were on the verge of being airsick, were nearly killed before they got buckled up.

"Thank you," I told him. "I have a new respect for pilots."

"Don't mention it," the colonel replied, and I was sure I knew what he meant.

Several hours later the colonel came back on, announcing, "We're descending to Hawaii." I was looking out the window of the left jump door, resting against it's curvature.

"Oh, great!" the colonel called out. "We have a 'door open' warning light."

WE'RE ALL MAD, YOU KNOW

I looked down and my knee had moved the opening lever slightly, but was enough to turn on his light. I closed it again quickly reporting, "It's okay, it was just me."

"That's about all the excitement I can take for one day airman!" the colonel shouted. "Sit down and buckle yourself up."

I did so quickly. A few moments later the navigator's head appeared from the cockpit. He was checking to see if I had obeyed the order, and the colonel came back on.

"You're free to move around the cabin, McGuire," he said. "Just take it easy."

Fifteen minutes later we were on the ground. We stayed at the Holiday Inn on Waikiki Beach. The island was so young that the beach hadn't turned to sand yet. The grains were large and sharp, making it hard to walk on. When I saw the club named Davy Jones Locker, I knew it had to be my kind of place. The inside was a scene from an old Spanish galleon. A huge, six foot deep salt water aquarium adorned the entrance and could be seen from everywhere in the club. The island is more beautiful than a camera can give justice to.

Flying north out of Hawaii, there was a long silence in the 130. I had been looking out the left scanner's window. The Colonel keyed his mike, "Those are some mighty hard clouds down there," he said calmly. We were following the Aleutian Islands chain, and those clouds were snow capped mountains.

It's said that flying is hours of sheer boredom, separated by moments of sheer terror. Things happen fast when you get close to the ground. We were on final approach to Elmandorf AFB, Alaska. The check list read "gear down."

"Did they get down?" the pilot asked.

"I can't tell," the engineer replied. "Could be that the lights are just out."

"I'm going to raise the gear and lower them again," the pilot said. We were on short final barely one hundred feet off the ground. Everyone was paying special attention to the whine of the hydraulic systems. There was a distinctive thump as the gear locked down, followed by another distinctive, and reassuring, thump as the wheels touched the runway only a moment later. They say any landing you walk away from is a good landing. This one happened at 0300 and the sun was just setting on a mid-summer day. Three hours later, it would be up again.

I rented a car and drove seventy-five miles north, completely overwhelmed. Alaska is indeed a huge frontier. The return flight to Okinawa was nonstop and in a straight line.

Some regulation required that the boat be painted, but we couldn't find anybody to paint it. Vic sent me to get the paint. Red for the deck and white for the hull. "Give me some of that blue," I said to the requisition sergeant. "I'm gonna three-tone it."

I put the blue below the water line and I liked it. I thought it looked sharp. Vic couldn't believe it. Nate came out to see it. He looked, not saying a word and then went back inside. The squadron commander, my friend the Lt. Colonel, and the squadron first sergeant came out next. Still nobody talked. Later, in Nate and Vic's office, Vic told me that what I had done was strictly against regulations. Nate couldn't hold a straight face any longer and spreading a wide smile concluded, "The old man liked it." The boat remained red, white and blue.

The weather on Okinawa is unpredictable, and typhoons play havoc with the island. Following one such typhoon, we drew a mission.

I knew as we headed for the airplane that this would not be a routine flight. I was on alert, and we were being scrambled.

"Any chance that we're going to war?" I asked my partner, a veteran PJ named Randy McComb.

"There's always that chance," he answered.

Our first idea of what was going on came during the pilot's briefing after the C-130 was already in the air. They typhoon had capsized a freighter, and a few survivors were clinging to a life raft.

"I hope you guys are ready," the pilot said as we reached the scene. "If we find anybody alive, you're going in."

McComb pushed his mike away from his mouth and pulled my helmet away from my ear. "Just let them try to keep us in this plane!" he yelled over the roar of the engines. I gave him the "thumb's up."

Two hours of scanning in an organized grid failed to reveal anything more than some floating debris.

"Something yellow at ten o'clock," Randy reported calmly. The airplane banked left.

Suddenly I was hungry. If I was going out into this stormy ocean, it was going to be on a full stomach. I opened a green C-ration can and began to wolf down some chow. I stopped chewing as I watched over Randy's shoulder at the upside-down life raft as it passed under the aircraft.

"We'll look awhile longer," the pilot said over the intercom. But no matter how hard we searched, we found nothing. This typhoon proved to be a killer that claimed many lives. Some perished right below us, and there was nothing we could do about it.

Patrick Fitzpatrick, one of our Kadena PJs, got to be the hero. He was lowered to a Greek freighter to tend a seriously ill sailor. The weather worsened, making a pick-up impossible. For three days, Fitz stayed on board with the casualty, keeping an IV open for fluid replacement, and injecting drugs. He was in constant radio contact with an MD.

Later, Nate read us a letter from the ship's captain and showed us a three hundred dollar check made out to Fitz. The money was returned to the sailors, and two weeks later a floatation ring was delivered to us that bore the ship's name. This gift we kept, and it was hung beside the other trophys that adorned the section's walls.

Two activities occupied most of our free time: free fall parachuting and SCUBA diving. A Marine colonel that had won the Medal of Honor in Vietnam was the parachute club's president. It took an act of Congress to allow us to use Marine Corps aircraft for sport jumping on Saturdays, but the Medal of Honor carries a lot of clout.

We met one morning at Naha airport, loading into the baggage compartment of an OV-10 Bronco recon plane.

WE'RE ALL MAD, YOU KNOW

Four jumpers could fit back to back in the snug, smooth-walled compartment. The first man out had only a strap to hold on to. When the plane took off all four of us slid toward the rear. We were held in only by one strap. Had it broken, we would have fallen out onto the runway.

Over the drop zone, we stowed the strap and waited. At ten thousand feet, the pilot gave the plane full throttle and nosed her nearly straight up. We slid out of the airplane, completely out of control, and tumbled in free fall. It was great. Once on the ground we repacked our 'chutes and climbed on a Marine CH-46 helicopter for our next lift. The jump club's motto was, "It's a beautiful day to die." We had to take this concept lightly because we came so close to actually doing it so often.

The water around Okinawa was crystal clear and comfortably warm. Most of our free time dives stayed above sixty feet to give us an hour of bottom time. My best friend and fellow PJ, Jeff McVey, kept after me to make a deep dive with him. So one day four of us drove northeast for fifteen miles to find an unpopulated stretch of cliffs. Below was the Pacific Ocean crashing into the rocks. Packing our gear down a narrow path, we entered the ocean at a sandy patch surrounded by boulders. We entered the ocean carrying our fins and fighting the waves until we were chest deep. We sat on the bottom to put our fins on with waves rolling over our heads and the surge rolling and tossing us about. As we began the dive, the bottom fell away quickly. At twenty feet the wave surge no longer affected us. At forty feet a sheer cliff dropped away and we floated down the side of the wall, bottoming out at one hundred fifteen feet. The bottom continued to slope down and was littered with boulders that thinned out as we went deeper. Visibility was decreasing rapidly past one hundred forty feet and my ears began to ring. When we hit one hundred seventy-five feet we decided that was deep enough. My ears were ringing loudly from nitrogen narcosis and I told myself not to succumb to its effects. But that's about like drinking a fifth of booze and telling yourself not to get drunk.

One of us found a Coke bottle and thought it would be really neat to have a Coke break while we were twice as deep under the ocean as any recreational diver is allowed to go. On the edge of hallucinating, we took turns removing our regulators and drinking sea water out of it until we emptied the bottle. The visibility at this depth was not much better than twenty feet. The bottom sloped away steeply to an inky unknown. Shadowy things moved in the boundary between dark and black. I convinced myself that they were more effects of nitrogen narcosis.

We stayed on the bottom for twenty minutes. As we began making our slow ascent to the surface, the water began to get lighter and clearer. At twenty feet, our first decompression stop, the water appeared as clear as glass compared to the depths below us. We stayed for five minutes before stopping again at ten feet. It's boring but it beats getting "bent." We swam toward shore at this depth, decompressing as we swam. We had to kill twenty minutes anyway to complete our decompression. None of us got the bends.

We didn't always take our SCUBA gear. The same four of us would take two spear guns and swim out to depths of thirty to forty feet and take turns going down. We could spend over a minute and a half on the bottom before returning to the surface. We'd take our catch to a road side burger stand and trade it for food.

Sometimes you just want to get drunk. There's no good reason for it, and you didn't do it often, but for some reason it just had to be done. On those occasions, we went to the "Bear's Blue Bucket."

The "Bucket" was tiny. There was only room for about eight full-size Americans in the joint. The only thing served was hot sake.

We called the mama-san who ran the place "Bear" because of the wrinkles in her aging face. The rest of the name came from the fact that at the end of the bar was a blue bucket, used for patrons who had too much to drink. Bear didn't mind cleaning it out after being used, but she got really pissed if you lost it on her bar.

The Bear had survived World War II. Just barely. She had been rescued by some GIs moments before she was to throw herself off Suicide Cliffs, where many Ryukyans lost their lives after being told that Americans would kill and eat them.

The Blue Bucket was only one of the many small bars on Okinawa, but for some of us PJs, it was our second home in times of need.

The PJ network was a global community. If one needed help, he could count on all of us to do what we could. Word came out to us one day that a PJ somewhere was in trouble.

205

Nate scheduled a meeting so that as many PJs as possible could attend. Nate told us who the PJ was, and a little about the problem.

"I know this PJ," Nate said. "He's getting the short end of the stick. I want to know who will stand beside me on this one?"

He took off his beret and threw it on his desk, casting his "vote" that he was "in," and challenging the rest of us to do the same.

You could have heard the proverbial pin drop. It took a moment for me to remember all of the times these magnificent men had stood up for me. My beret was the first to come out of my jungle fatigue pocket and land on top of Nate's.

Three more landed soon after, and every few seconds another. When Randy McComb took his out, he looked at it for a moment, then at Nate. He let his fly.

"You're all crazy!" shouted one veteran PJ who didn't agree with the vote. "You younger guys I can understand, but McComb...and you, Carmichale. Don't you realize what you're doing?" He turned his attention to Nate. "I want a transfer."

"Consider it done" Nate answered.

Nate stood up. "I'm going to see the old man."

He left, leaving his beret at the bottom of the pile.

He was gone about half an hour. The "vet" had left to pack his bags by the time Nate returned.

"Pick up your beret," Nate ordered. "They've dropped the charges.

It was better to find out that one member didn't fit in with the team this way, than to find out during a mission later in some jungle or in the middle of the ocean. Even though he was a capable and brave PJ, he didn't fit in with our team.

A slow down in TDYs gave Nate time to re-certify me on the HH-53, six months after he had intended to. We really had been just too busy. The H-3 would still have to wait. Pappy had come to Okinawa, but I had been away TDY and missed him. My next APR was due and I was happy to receive mostly sevens. They said Pappy was satisfied and even laughed when he saw the boat. He left a message for me to attach a cork to the boat key and paint it red.

A Military Airlift Command general dropped in one evening. He said he just wanted to visit for a minute with some of his PJs and picked me out for a picture. He asked me if everything was OK, and you could feel everyone in the room holding their breath.

"It does seem I've been wearing two stripes for a long time," I mentioned.

"I'll look into that, airman McGuire," he promised. I noticed his aides taking notes. For two weeks I was kidded about asking the top brass for a promotion, but two weeks was all it took before I was wearing three stripes and people were calling me sergeant.

The promotion also meant that I had to attend Non-Commissioned Officer's Leadership School. I told Nate that I didn't really want to attend this school. He thought that I should, and suggested that I think about it awhile longer. Shortly before the school started, Nate called me in.

"I need an answer, Gary. This paperwork has to be hand carried today, or the slot will be filled by somebody else." He was giving me every opportunity, but I couldn't see the big picture.

"Do I have to?" I asked him.

"I've never had to give you an order yet, McGuire. Don't make me start now."

If that wasn't an order, then I'd never heard one. I signed the paper.

The class was held at Kadena, but people came from all over the Far East for this school. I was required to live in the barracks with the rest of the class. The school lasted one month, was very military, and we weren't allowed to leave the barracks even on weekends unless the entire class went. Near the end of the class, a PJ came to get me.

"There's a party at Nate's house tonight and he wants you to be there. I've come to get you," he said.

"But the rules?" I questioned.

"Pappy's there," he replied. That's all he needed to say.

The atmosphere was not very party like. People were drinking light and talking about the future. Pappy said he knew I had it in me and that I hadn't disappointed him. He told me he was retiring and that Nate, Vic and many others would be transferred within the next six months. "I don't know how things will go for you when we're gone," he said. "But there is something I want you to do for me. I need for you to extend here for six months to give the next administration time to settle in with all the new crews to get certified. They'll be short handed for a few months. You'll be able to leave here and get an early out."

It sounded as if he knew something that he wasn't saying. He was putting the mission above all personal considerations just the way you expect a professional to act. I wasn't about to be any different.

"Of course I will, Pappy," I said, not knowing what trouble awaited me when my allies were gone. The deadline for me to apply for an extension was well past, but that was no obstacle for Pappy.

Saying good-bye to Pappy for the last time that night nearly brought tears to my eyes. He was one in a million.

Several students witnessed my leaving the barracks and wanted to know why I could come and go when nobody else could. The instructor told them what I was going to say, "Because he's a PJ, that's why!"

I received a message from Vic a few days later. It said, "Study your H-3E manual. You're scheduled for a flight the same day you get back."

Again I left the barracks, this time to get my manuals. When I returned, those that saw me were angry. I ignored them. The few friends I made there thought it was fun to know someone that didn't have to always follow the rules.

My first orientation flight on an H-3E turned into my check ride. I answered all the questions right the first time and performed my duties well. Vic said he had never certified anyone on their first flight before. I was scheduled for a flight on the 3-E to Taiwan for the following day.

It was supposed to be a two day TDY and fly back for the pilots cross country flight requirement. The co-pilot was a second lieutenant on his first flight to Taiwan. The pilot had been explaining details that meant nothing to me until he said, "There's an island fifteen miles south of here. It has a small runway and is the only place to land between Okinawa and Taiwan." We flew on for a few minutes then the pilot said, "We don't have anything better to do, let's go look at it." He then banked the helicopter hard left.

We flew in a circle around the island at three hundred feet. There was a small town, a few fields and a tiny runway. "No place to vacation," the co-pilot mentioned. We flew out over the water gaining altitude. Five minutes out at seven thousand feet, the #1 engine failed. We dropped like a rock as the pilot pulled the stick as high as it would go and banked left heading back to the island. The best he could do was slowly lose altitude, because it couldn't fly on it's single good engine. The glide path put us down right on the runway.

"This may be no place to vacation," the pilot said, "but it beats setting this bird down in the water."

I couldn't have agreed more. Training for the worst is one thing, having to survive it is another.

To solve the problem, a 130 had to land with a spare engine and a repair crew. The new problem was that the Japanese government wouldn't allow that heavy of an airplane to land on the little runway. It took Henry Kissinger two days to get permission. Meanwhile, I thought I was going to starve. Americanized Oriental food is pretty good. The real thing is not edible. Things smelled of burnt eggshells. Some of it was slimy. I would have eaten it when I got hungry enough, but thank God the C-rations on the helicopter didn't run out until the day we left. We did drink our share of Sake and Santora whiskey.

WE'RE ALL MAD, YOU KNOW

We left the island on the C-130 that brought the engine and crew in. We were informed that a C-130 crashed at Kadena, killing the entire crew. It wasn't a rescue aircraft, but a crew is a crew, whatever the mission. The burned out fuselage was still on the ground off the runway when we landed.

Death was a fact of life we lived with daily. Pararescue duty killed one PJ per month on average. Some months would go by with no one being killed. One month we lost six. We had a one-in-three hundred chance of dying in any given month. I had come close too often. The PJ that flew with me to Okinawa from the States broke his leg on a jump one day, bad enough to ground him permanently. Death is a sadder event, but not much. It was heart wrenching to watch him turn in his equipment and clear out his locker. Even more so to see him standing there in shoes, straight leg pants and no beret. I got a call from the supply sergeant a few days later. He said that a watch I had requested some months earlier was available now.

"It belonged to a PJ that got hurt," the sergeant said as I signed for it. I still have that watch to this day. I felt the government owed me that much.

I watched every PJ in the place take their turn manning the remote rescue station at Ching Chuan Kang Air Base in Taiwan. My name was the last on the duty roster list on the schedule board, and my heart sank the day it was erased. The base was being permanently closed.

But a last minute decision kept it open for one more month. I had two days to get ready for a three-week TDY.

211

WE'RE ALL MAD, YOU KNOW

Fred Scantling, the PJ I trained with at Hill, was already there. He said he told everybody about the smoke we shared the night we jumped into Utah Lake. Now we were closing a chapter in history together. We thought it was fitting, although we also thought they should have sent in a couple of big names and made a big deal out of it. It was a big deal, but it slipped into history unnoticed...or would have, had I not been arrested.

It happened during the last weekend we were there. We were partying in town with two lieutenants that piloted the Jolly Green. Officers and enlisted men don't normally pal around together, but nothing else we did was normal, so why should this be any different?

"Town" was ten klicks away, and one bar in particular had been known to slip GIs a mickey. It insured that the GI wouldn't resist while he was being robbed. This way no one got hurt, and the only things missing were a few dollars.

After a few drinks I felt funny. I thought maybe I just needed to take a leak.

Three locals followed me into the restroom. The room started spinning and my fingers and toes began to grow numb.

"Fred," I yelled, trying to overcome the strains of "Free Bird" blaring over the sound system. "I'm going outside to get some fresh air."

"Don't be gone too long," he yelled back. We didn't worry about each other because we were PJs, and could take care of ourselves. That's how cocky we were.

The fresh air wasn't as fresh as I was hoping for. There was always an open "Benjo" ditch nearby reeking of human sewage. I decided to stay in the light, trusting my intuition. The last thing I remembered was leaning against a pillar outside of the "hotel," which was actually a brothel. Then my feet slid out from under me.

"Hey, wake up! Come on, get on your feet!" I felt someone lifting me by the arms. When I opened my eyes, I could see two burly sky cops. The next thing I knew, I was being dragged toward a paddy wagon.

"Stand on your own, sergeant," ordered one. I locked my knees and was able to stand.

"I need your ID and gate pass."

I surrendered the two cards. He began reading me my "rights." Halfway through, I interupted him.

"Wait a minute. This sounds like I'm under arrest," I protested.

"You are."

"You don't seem to understand, I'm not drunk."

"You're not only drunk, you're public drunk."

"I'm also a PJ, and this won't look good to my NCOIC," I slurred, as if that made any difference to him.

"Well, PJ, do you want me to add 'resisting arrest' to the public drunk charge?"

It became obvious to me that this guy wasn't just an asshole, he was an ass's hole.

The next thing I knew was that I was in the van. Then I fell to sleep.

I woke suddenly with one of those eerie sensations that I was being watched. I believe that the mind receives more than we are consciously aware of, and this was one of those times. I looked out the window and saw Fred standing not far away. He had a concerned look on his face.

"Fred!" I yelled. His expression changed to "where the hell did that come from."

"Fred!" I yelled louder.

He turned toward my voice and saw me inside the wagon. His face lit up for an instant at having found me, then frowned because of where he found me.

"Get me the hell out of here!" I yelled through the glass.

He marched up to the van and opened the back doors.

"Do you have your ID?" Fred asked cooly.

"No, That's the first thing they wanted."

It was just as well, too, because the sky cops were running toward us with their pistols drawn. They told us that if we had have made a break for it, they would have gunned us down. Sky cops take their jobs too damned seriously.

They did, however, have enough respect for pararescue not to charge Fred with an escape attempt. I said "good night" to Fred and was driven back to base for lock up.

A major from Kadena was the TDY squadron commander. He was at the cop shop waiting for me and took me directly into his custody.

"I hope you realize that you just created a great deal of paperwork for me," he said as he drove me to quarters.

"Yes, sir, and I'm real sorry for that."

"Yeah, well, I'm supposed to restrict you to base and I have to recommend that you attend alcohol rehab when we get back to Kadena. Here." He handed me back my ID and gate pass.

WE'RE ALL MAD, YOU KNOW

"I really do apologize for bothering you so late, major. Thank's for bailing my ass out."

"Hell, there's no way I'd leave a PJ in any brig anywhere." He looked at me in typical GI demeanor. "I know there won't be any more trouble out of you."

He was right. But I did go back off base. After all, I had a gate pass.

Everything the Air Force wanted from the Taiwan air base was dismantled and taken away. We flew the last sortie as the last operational unit to ever depart Ching Chuan Kang Air Base, Taiwan. There was no fanfare, no brass bands, nothing. We simply left.

Few would ever know that we were ever there in the first place.

Eighteen months is a long time, but it flew by before any of us were ready. I had been Nate's Pinochle partner and we were unbeatable. I loved this man and he was transferring out. In all, fourteen PJs were being replaced. These would be our last few days together. Nate locked the doors early for the second time, and we drank Harvey Wallbangers from the Igloo. This was no ordinary rotation. It was the end of an era. The day Nate left, everyone had a lump in their throats-- mine escalated into tears. One-by-one they left. These wonderful, heroic men that I had had the pleasure and honor to call my friends. They all shared the same concern for what would happen to me under the new NCOIC.

One story that can't be left out is the last sortie of Tail Number 777.

215

WE'RE ALL MAD, YOU KNOW

777 was an HH-3E Jolly Green Giant rescue helicopter. She flew in combat before coming to Okinawa, and suffered the indignity of being painted silver.

There's something testosterone about the way pilots feel about their aircraft, and the retirement of 777 was a big deal, complete with the top brass from the squadron, photographers, and champagne. Each of the crewmembers were handed a glass of bubbly, and as we bid a fond farewell to the old gal, base sirens began to howl. It was a genuine cry of dispair, from machines that said something special to a special machine.

We couldn't drink the champagne. We simply had to say good-bye to a trusty old member of "the team."

That damn APR.

From the first day, I was treated like the worst PJ in history.

"So you're Gary McGuire," the new NCOIC said sarcastically. He mostly ignored me. He fired me as the SCUBA section chief and hired a long time friend of his. He tried to make it easy saying I was simply outranked. I remembered Pappy Lacasse. He asked me to help them in the transition and in loyalty to him I did the best I could, but the wind was out of my sails. Any thought of making this a life-long career was out the window. I would never be accepted again. Pappy and Nate knew my fate a long time ago. They shared some of the hurt for me. I'm sure they felt it very deeply. My last few months were agonizing, but still I didn't want to leave. I wanted things back the way they were. Life doesn't work that way. I had only two friends left when I got on the airplane headed back for the States. They were glad to see me go, for my own sake.

I was supposed to go to San Francisco to out-process, but I had some relatives in LA and since that's where my plane landed, I figured I might as well stay a few days with them. My cousin there was my age and he and I partied heavy. He even drove me to San Francisco to out-process. Once on base, we had to ask directions. The airman giving directions couldn't take his eye off my beret. My cousin commented later that people seemed to be in awe of me.

"It's been this way for nearly four years," I told him, "but it's all over now."

The sergeant I reported to started to give me a hard time for being AWOL for the past three days, and for being late today, then noticed the word Pararescue on my orders.

"You PJs are all alike," he said. "I'll just take those days off the leave you have coming."

It took the better part of the day to finish the paper work and I was just leaving when a female voice screamed from a room down the hall, "Where's that PJ?"

She came running out looking with wide eyes. "There you are. Where do you think you're going?" She tried to talk me into joining the reserves. "Do you know how rarely we see any of you guys?" she said, as if maybe I didn't, and started to go on when I stopped her.

"There are things you can't possibly know," I told her, "but thank you very much just the same."

"If you quit now you'll be a has-been for the rest of your life," she scolded.

WE'RE ALL MAD, YOU KNOW

That almost did the trick. I thought back on the long months of training, seeing the faces of so few who meant so much. I thought about the importance of the mission and the prestige of the uniform. I thought about how much I was going to miss this.

"It's better to be a 'has been,'" I told her, "than a 'never was.'"

I turned around and walked...no, marched...out of the United States Air Force.

The PJ

So you want to be, I heard you say, a PJ.
One in ten thousand to wear the maroon beret.
You want to run, jump, swim, and climb,
To save a life in the nick of time.
Into the Air Force you did join,
To serve your country, and be adorned.
You are not at all wanted by this elite corps
Of three hundred men, heroes and more.
You are told of the legacy,
And of your life expectancy.
You're pushed beyond your own endurance
To test your heart for your partner's assurance.
Through the pipeline of classes that last a year,
You struggle through and conquer your fear.
The finest equipment at your disposal
To get you where you can be useful.
There is no one to thank you for your strife.
Only the few that mourn you when you lose your life.
So you want to be, I heard you say, a PJ...
One in ten thousand to wear the maroon beret.

Gary W. McGuire

ORDER FORM

To: Mary Lee Press
      PO Box 295
      Chandler, OK 74834

Please ship to me at the address shown below the following number of copies of *We're All Mad, You Know*. Enclosed is my check or money order for $_____ which includes $2.50 (each)[1] for shipping and handling. (Oklahoma residents add .65 @ book state sales tax).

_____ copies @ $11.95 each $_____

Shipping and Handling @ $2.50 ea.   _____

Oklahoma Sales Tax (OK only)   _____

TOTAL AMOUNT ENCLOSED   _____

Ship to:

Name_____

Address_____

City _____

State _____ Zip _____

Telephone (   ) _____

---

[1] Bulk orders will be shipped at standard rates as specified by customer.